Unholy Treasure

Palmyrton Estate Sale Mystery Series, Volume 10

S.W. Hubbard

Published by S.W. Hubbard, 2023.

UNHOLY TREASURE

First edition. December 30, 2023.

Copyright © 2023 S.W. Hubbard.

ISBN: 979-8874097066

Written by S.W. Hubbard.

Chapter 1

A bright beam of October morning sunlight slices through the gap in my bedroom drapes illuminating the face of my sleeping husband beside me. At 6:30, the house is quiet. Miraculously, our twins are still asleep, and even my dog Ethel snores peacefully at the foot of the bed.

Years have passed since I've enjoyed the luxury of sitting alone at the kitchen table to drink my first cup of coffee. I slip carefully out from under the covers, and although Ethel snuffles a bit, she doesn't rise to follow me. Tiptoeing past the twins' bedroom, I descend to the kitchen and flip the switch on the coffeemaker, which Sean set up the night before. As I wait for the coffee to brew, I reflexively reach for my phone and realize it's upstairs charging next to my bed. I'm not going to risk rousing everyone to retrieve it, so I sit down and content myself with looking out the sliding doors to my backyard. What a strange sensation to not be checking email, scrolling through social media, or reading depressing news stories.

Stillness doesn't come easily to me. As a working mother of two toddlers, I've always got half my brain focused on my estate sale business and the other half anticipating the life-risking antics my children will come up with next. I pour my coffee and empty my mind of to-do lists. As I watch yellow leaves drifting down from our gingko tree, a visitor enters the backyard: a beautiful red fox.

He's about the size of Ethel but moves with the slinky grace of a cat, crossing the yard as if it's the African savannah not New Jersey suburbia. As he reaches Sean's herb garden, he pauses and turns his pointy nose toward the window. Our gazes meet. Unimpressed by my tousled hair and shapeless flannel pants, he shakes his fluffy red and black tail to illustrate truly elegant morning attire.

"Hello, beautiful," I murmur. But he's not up for interspecies communication and scurries off in search of his breakfast.

For a moment, I feel a pang of regret that I was the only one to enjoy this encounter with nature. Then I remember that if everyone had been awake,

Ethel would have been barking her head off and the twins would've been beating their fists against the glass.

I accept that the fox was my morning gift but feel that now I really should begin doing something productive with this quiet time. Not quite ready to tackle spreadsheets on my laptop, I settle for sorting the mail, which we haven't collected from the box at the curb for several days. I slip out the front door, hoping none of my neighbors see me in my pajamas. But as I scoop three days' worth of catalogs, solicitations, and political flyers into my arms, Reilly the Yorkshire terrier and his owner appear at my side.

I can never remember the owner's name, but it's hard to forget Reilly because Ethel detests him. In her eyes, his canine sins are unforgiveable—1) he's yappy, 2) he gets his fur styled, and 3) he wears jackets.

Today Reilly is adorned in red tartan plaid with his whiskers trimmed in a doggie goatee. "Good morning, Reilly." I inject my voice with extra enthusiasm in hopes that his owner won't notice that I'm not greeting him by name.

"Good morning, Audrey," the owner says. "I see you've had some visitors."

Only then do I notice that the three potted chrysanthemums I had arranged at the base of my mailbox in a fit of HGTV nest-building have been shorn of their red and gold flowers. They now look like army recruits who've just received their basic training buzz cuts. Did my beautiful fox friend do this?

"Oh, no! What happened?"

"Deer," Reilly's owner explains, as the dog lifts his leg and contemptuously irrigates the stumps of my autumn display. "They love mums. Guess you didn't spray them, huh?"

"Spray the deer? Am I supposed to stand guard with a hose?"

"Spray the flowers with Deer-Off," my neighbor explains with the elaborate patience of a kindergarten teacher. "It keeps Bambi and her crew away as long as you remember to reapply after every rain."

All up and down the block I see that everyone's mums are blooming brilliantly. Chalk up another Martha Stewart fail for Audrey Nealon. Am I the only person who didn't get the memo on this deer spray stuff?

"Maybe this new deer hunting program will help us hang onto our azaleas and tulips come spring." Reilly's human takes a step back and squints at me. "You're not one of those anti-hunting protesters, are you?"

"I haven't been to a protest since college," I assure him. "What's the controversy?"

"Palmyrton is allowing limited deer hunting in Alexander Hamilton Park to cull the herd, and all the animal rights people are out there picketing trying to stop the hunt."

I'm hardly a PETA activist, but Palmyrton is too densely populated for hunting. "Men with hunting rifles are going to be shooting in the Hamilton Park forest? If I lived near the park, I'd sure be nervous about that! You can see houses from the hiking trails."

"Bow hunting only," my neighbor assures me. "And they're hand-picking the hunters, not just throwing open the park to every yahoo with a weapon." He pulls Reilly closer on his leash. "The town has to do something to control the deer population. Still, Reilly and I won't be walking in Hamilton Park until this hunt is over, will we boy?"

"I SAW A FOX IN MY BACKYARD this morning," I tell my assistant Ty when I arrive at the office at nine.

A sly grin splits his handsome, dark face. "I saw a fox this morning too, but she wasn't clear out in the yard."

Ty's love life is the stuff of legend. At thirty, he shows no sign of settling down, unlike my other assistant, Donna, who's currently vacationing with her boyfriend in Greece. I'm expecting she might come home engaged.

Before I can pump Ty on the details of the newest woman in his life, there's a knock on our office door.

Isabelle Trent, Palmyrton's most successful Realtor, breezes into my office in her flawless black pant suit, offering air kisses all around. Ty moves a box of dusty books off our visitor's chair and, to her credit, Isabelle only hesitates for a split second before sitting down.

"I have a wonderful opportunity for you, Audrey," she begins in her trademark upbeat Realtor's voice.

"Oh?" Immediately, I'm on guard. Since real estate and estate sales are adjacent fields, Isabelle is both a friend and a business associate. She's often recommended me to clients who need help clearing their homes before putting them on the market. But those referrals usually come via a quick phone call or text message. It's quite unusual for Isabelle to stop by my office just to tell me about a client who needs an estate sale organizer.

Ty seems equally suspicious. He's working at his desk, but clearly keeping an ear tuned to the conversation.

"I'm about to list a fa-a-a-bulous home—the house of the architect Gaston Dupree." She pauses for my response and gets none. "Did you know he lived right here in Palmer County?"

"Uhm...since I don't know who he is, I definitely didn't know he lived here," I reply.

Isabelle elevates her perfectly shaped brows. "Gaston Dupree is one of the heirs of mid-century modern architects like Eero Saarinen and Philip Johnson. He designed an exquisite house for himself and his family on a lot that backs up to Hamilton Park. Hiking trails are only a quarter mile away, yet most people aren't even aware of the house. That's how perfectly it was designed to blend with its surroundings." Isabelle clasps her hands to her heart. "Truly, it's magnificent."

"So why's he gettin' rid of it?" Ty asks, giving voice to my precise thought.

"Sadly, Gaston Dupree died suddenly last year. His widow is handicapped—she uses a wheelchair—and it's become increasingly difficult for her to live alone even though the house is barrier-free. So her children have persuaded her to sell and move into assisted living."

This sad story is an everyday occurrence in our line of work, so I'm still not seeing why Isabelle has made a personal appearance to discuss this job. "It sounds like the kind of house we'd love to organize a sale for—" I begin.

"Oh, it is! Full of lovely art from around the world and furniture custom designed for Dupree. The man knew everyone in the art and design world."

I can't stand it anymore. "I'm sensing a complication here, Isabelle."

She smoothes her perfect hair and brushes a nonexistent speck from her pants. "Yes, well...Mrs. Dupree has requested assistance in the matter of the caretaker's cottage on the property. The gentleman who lived there was a family friend—a rather eccentric fellow—and he too has recently passed away, so that home also needs to be cleared."

"Hold up!" Ty interrupts. "Eccentric is code for hoarder. Ain't no way we're doin' another hoarder house, Isabelle."

Ever since the horrific consequences of our project clearing the house of Harold the Hoarder, we've all been extremely wary of houses filled with clutter. "If we have to take a hoarder job to get the good job, I'm not sure we're willing to go there, Isabelle."

"Hoarder? Oh, no—Mr. Singleterry wasn't a hoarder. The house is quite spartan, really. It's just that his children are apparently rather troubled, and they haven't come forward to take away their father's possessions. Mrs. Dupree is the executor of his estate in addition to being his landlord. So we'd need you to hold a sale there as well as at the big house."

Ty and I exchange a glance. "Ok-a-a-y. So what's the complication?"

Isabelle clears her throat. "Mrs. Dupree wants to find a way to give Mr. Singleterry's heirs a little cash without it looking like a handout. So she wants to divert some of the proceeds from her sale and assign them to Mr. Singleterry's sale. I told her I'd enquire. I don't think it's illegal, is it? After all, she wants to give them more than their fair share."

"Hmmm. I think I'd like to discuss this directly with Mrs. Dupree before I decide," I say.

"Of course!" Isabelle jumps up. "Can you stop by tomorrow? She's always home. I need to get this settled so I can move forward with listing the house."

"Sure. Tell her we'll be there at ten."

Isabelle gives me the address and sails out.

Ty scowls at the closing door. "Sounds like a tax dodge to me."

Chapter 2

I arrive home from work early to find my twins happily playing in the family room while our nanny Roseline folds laundry and keeps the peace. "Mama!" they shriek in unison, rushing to meet me. Aiden trips over the dog and crashes into his sister, resulting in two crying toddlers at my feet.

So much for contentment.

I sink onto the floor to hug them, and their tears are soon forgotten. "Two books," Thea announces, depositing the colorful volumes in my lap.

"We went to the library today," Roseline says. "Returned last week's books and took out a new batch. Except for the big trucks book. Aiden wouldn't give it up, so the librarian said we could renew it."

"Tucks!" Aiden drags his favorite into our "to be read" pile.

"I've gotta buy him his own copy," I tell Roseline. "He can't keep the library copy checked out until he leaves for college."

"As soon as you buy him that book, he'll lose interest in trucks and move on to dinosaurs," Roseline predicts. As she gathers together her belongings to leave for the day, Sean arrives home from his job as a Palmyrton police department detective.

Sean's entrance sends the kids into a second paroxysm of joy. From me, they want hugs and cuddles and snuggling with books. From Sean, they want action. They climb all over him, treating him like a human jungle gym. He's a horse, a bear, a train, a swing.

Typically, they could go on like this for an hour, but I notice Sean slowing down after twenty minutes. He's still giving horsey rides on his leg, but he seems rather distracted.

I encourage the kids to toss nerf balls into a basket and curl up next to Sean on the sofa. "What's wrong? Hard day at work?"

He massages his temples. "Would you mind getting me some ibuprofen?"

For my man of steel, this is like asking for a blood transfusion. I leap up to get the pills. "Are you sick?"

"No. My head's been pounding since the staff meeting with our new chief."

The Chief of Police that Sean has worked under since joining the Palmyrton police department recently retired, and everyone is having a hard time getting used to the new guy. "What did he do this time?" I ask.

Sean leans his head back on the sofa and props his feet on the coffee table. "He's obsessed with crime data. He announced all detectives have to work a night shift patrolling downtown Palmyrton because we've experienced a 200% increase in muggings since July."

"Really? That's an alarming jump, isn't it?"

Sean rolls his eyes. "Not if you actually understand statistics. We went from one mugging in July to three muggings in September. It's just a seasonal blip, not a violent crime wave. In mid-summer, people are all down at the shore, and the muggers follow the action there. In the fall, people come back, and we see a slight increase in street crime here. It happens every year."

"Did anyone point that out to the new chief?"

"Hoo, yeah. Poor Bill Reynolds. And he got his head cut off and served on a platter." Sean picks up an errant nerf ball and lobs it over Aiden's head into the basket. "Chief Gaskill just wants to score points with the mayor. He's already sent out a press release on his new crime-busting initiative."

There's nothing Sean hates more than grandstanding. I don't foresee a happy future with his new boss. "When do you have to serve your patrol shift?"

"This Friday. I'll probably be out until after 3:00 AM. It takes a full hour to make sure all the drunks have staggered home safely after closing time."

I say nothing. We had planned a family outing to the Bronx Zoo this Saturday since it's a rare weekend when I don't have a sale. But we can't get off to an early start if Sean has to work until the middle of the night. And if we leave late, the kids will miss their afternoon nap and get cranky.

Sean takes my hands in his. "I'm sorry, Audrey. I'm really disappointed, too."

I put on a cheery smile. "It's not your fault. You sleep in on Saturday, and we'll do something closer to home. The twins are probably too young to appreciate the Bronx Zoo anyway."

THE NEXT DAY, TY AND I go out to look at the Dupree house. "You heard from Donna at all?" Ty asks as he drives us out of Palmyrton.

"Yes, she texted me yesterday. They're in Mykonos now after leaving Athens, and then they're going to visit some of Alex's relatives in Paros." While we're stopped at a light, I pull out my phone to show Ty a photo of Donna and Alex in front of the Parthenon.

"Nice." But his voice doesn't sound very happy.

"What's the matter? You jealous?" Ty has always been protective of Donna because of the way her first husband abused her. But I thought he liked Alex Agyros as much as I do.

"Don't talk stupid," Ty says. "I'm just wonderin'—you think she'll come home engaged?"

"Possibly. That would be a good thing, wouldn't it? Donna would love to have a baby, and her clock is ticking."

"Yeah. Yeah, I guess." Ty's eyes dart to the GPS. "We gotta turn soon. You see the road?"

I point to a street sign partially hidden behind overgrown trees, and Ty makes a sharp left. The GPS seems to be leading us directly into the woods when suddenly, the narrow, paved road turns, and a long, low house made of wood, stone, and glass appears before us.

Ty whistles his approval. "No wonder Isabelle wettin' her pants over listin' this house. That's gotta be worth a few million."

We park in the driveway and follow a beautiful, gradually sloping flagstone walk leading to the wide front door. I'm halfway up it before it dawns on me that it's designed to accommodate Mrs. Dupree's wheelchair although it's certainly the most artistic ramp I've ever seen.

We ring the doorbell and seconds later the door swings inward as if opened by a ghost. Ty squints into the dim interior, then steps back as an electric wheelchair moves silently toward us. An elegant, silver-haired woman powers it forward with a slight movement of her curled right hand. "You must be Audrey and Ty. I'm Katherine Dupree. Come right in."

Her voice—melodic and strong—seems too forceful to be coming from such a frail body. Her wavy, silver hair is stylishly cut, and she wears subtle make-up and a tasteful cashmere sweater and pearls. She may be confined to a wheelchair, but she presents herself as a force to be reckoned with.

"I presume Isabelle has explained my situation here," she says. "Last year my husband died, and a few months ago, our old family friend who lived here on the property also passed." She sighs. "Without their support, it's become increasingly difficult for me to manage here at the house. I've had a series of home health aides, but they've all proved to be unreliable or...unsuitable... in one way or another. So I must leave this place."

Katherine's eyes grow glassy, but the tears don't spill over. A scrawny gray cat jumps into her lap. As Katherine strokes his rough fur, I notice he has only one eye. "I can't take any of my beautiful furniture with me, but at least I can take Louie," she says.

The cat jumps down and stalks toward me. When I bend down to pet him, he arches his back and hisses.

"Sorry. He's not friendly to anyone but me," Katherine explains. "I found him hiding under the big pine tree out front. Took me months to coax him indoors."

I give up on befriending the cat and begin looking around the house. The different areas of the main floor are defined by bookshelves, folding screens, and furniture placement. There are no doors or steps. The side and rear wall of the large open living space are solid glass. Today, the windows frame a riot of gold and red and orange. It feels like we're sitting right out in the woods.

"What a beautiful space," I say.

"Yes, I shall miss it, especially at this time of year. Autumn has always been my favorite season." Katherine rolls her chair closer to the window.

"Hey, look—there's two deer out there." Ty points to the well camouflaged forms of two doe picking their way delicately through the trees.

Katherine smiles. "Yes, my forest friends keep me company. Foxes, woodpeckers, wild turkeys...even the occasional bear." She scowls. "Unfortunately, the park service has started to permit bow hunting the deer in the park. They claim we have to cull the herd." She shudders. "I can't imagine killing those beautiful creatures."

Ty takes a step closer to the window and his brow draws down. "There's a man out there, too."

Katherine waves her hand and pivots away from the window with no concern. "Just a hiker. The trail in the park comes right up against our property line, so hikers cross onto my property all the time."

Chapter 3

Katherine Dupree turns away from the window to lead us on a tour of the house. Occasionally, there are empty spaces where a piece of furniture or a work of art appears to be missing. She notices me scrutinizing a large rectangular shadow on the wall above the dining table. "My children have taken a few items of significance to them. But neither of them lives in the type of home that could accommodate this furniture and these larger works of art." She lifts one delicate hand to wave at a painting as she glides past in the wheelchair. "And I certainly can't take it with me. So all of it will have to be sold. Isabelle told me you're an expert in finding buyers for unusual pieces."

Ty and I exchange a glance as Katherine powers along in front of us, leading us toward the bedrooms. I know what he's thinking: Mrs. Dupree seems remarkably unsentimental about the disposition of all her beautiful possessions. Often sales where the owner is downsizing to assisted living are one long tug of war over what can be taken and what must be sold. Katherine has already made up her mind that it all must go. Of course, that makes the sale easier for us. But her stoic release of all that she's held dear is terribly sad.

Finally, we arrive at a sunny, small room crammed with houseplants. Some are blooming brilliantly, while others droop and drop yellow leaves. "Do you think you can find takers for my plants?" Katherine asks. "My daughter wants to dump them all on the compost heap." She rolls up to a sad-looking fern and plucks off a yellow frond. "I enjoy taking plants that my friends have neglected and nursing them back to health."

She doesn't have to say more. I can understand that this hobby of taking in the wounded and sick and returning them to health would be powerful for someone with so many health struggles of her own.

Ty also understands. "Sure, there will be folks who want them. Plants are very popular at estate sales."

We trade a glance behind Katherine's back as she leads us back to the living room. Now that we've seen all the rooms in the house, I know this sale will be a blockbuster. I'm making mental notes of art dealers to call and regular customers who will be interested in certain pieces. I absolutely want to run the sale of Gaston and Katherine Dupree's house.

Time to tackle part two of the project.

I turn away from examining a lovely teak etagere. "Isabelle mentioned that you also want us to sell the contents of the caretaker's cottage." I end the statement with the upward lilt of a question.

"Yes." Katherine motors over to a large desk. "I'll give you the key to go out and look at it. I'm afraid I can't accompany you."

She says nothing about the special terms, so I decide Ty and I should look at the cottage before I bring it up.

Katherine lets us out the back door and we follow a wide walkway through the woods to a tiny cottage with cedar shake siding, mullioned windows, and a stone chimney.

Ty sizes it up while I unlock the front door. "Looks like somethin' outta Hansel and Gretel."

Like the big house, the first floor here is one open space although much smaller.

"Dupree wasn't much for walls," I say.

"Musta been absent that day in architecture school." Ty does a 360-degree rotation in the middle of the room. "Isabelle didn't lie. The place is neat and clean—just a little dust on the furniture."

Crammed bookshelves line the walls on either side of the fireplace. A sturdy oak table with two chairs seems to have served double duty as a desk and a dining spot, as there is a solitary placemat at one end and an out-of-date desktop computer at the other. A cozy but worn easy chair with a floor lamp and an end table sit in front of the fire. Another chair with a view of a birdfeeder sits beside the window. A small entertainment center holds a CD player and scores of CDs. There's no TV.

Ty frowns and I can read his mind. Audio purists like vinyl records, but CDs are hard to sell. I scan the titles—Faure's Requiem, Mozart's Misa Brevis, lots of organ music. We'll be lucky to give them away.

The kitchen at the far end of the room is similarly spartan. One cabinet holds two plates, two bowls, two mugs, two glasses. Another holds a saucepan, a frying pan, and a baking pan. An open shelf displays some small wooden boxes and odd little pottery jars.

"Guess he didn't entertain." Ty heads upstairs, where we see a clean bathroom and a bedroom with a single bed and one dresser. An ornately carved wooden crucifix hangs over the bed. The closet holds five shirts and two pairs of khakis. A shelf attached to the wall holds a Bible and a framed photograph of three adults. I elbow Ty. "This is Gaston Dupree. I looked him up on Wikipedia last night."

Ty peers over my shoulder. "Looks like an old-time movie star."

Gaston faces the camera with a wide smile. He's tall and lean with a mane of wavy silver hair, straight, dark brows, and a strong chin. A younger Katherine leans on him, whether for physical support or affection isn't clear. The third person in the picture is a short, wiry man with a pugnacious tilt to his chin. "I guess that's Jefferson Singleterry."

"Weird that's the only picture in the house," Ty says. "You'd think he'd have some photos of his kids."

"That photo and the crucifix are the only decorative items."

Ty and I face each other. "There's hardly anything in this house," Ty says. "We could just bag it up and take it to the dump."

Together we troop downstairs.

I scratch my head. "Isabelle says Mrs. Dupree wants to find a way to funnel some money to Singleterry's heirs. But nothing here has any value. What would we say we sold that brought in a lot of cash?"

Ty scratches his head. "Guess you could say you found some valuable books and sold them to a dealer."

I cross the room to the bookshelves. All nonfiction—obscure titles regarding medieval history, the Crusades, lives of various saints. I suppose there could be something rare here. I pull a book off the shelf and open it. The margins of every page are covered in tiny, precise handwriting. "Ugh—he was a notetaker. That destroys all the value these books might have." I look longingly at Ty. "I really want the job at the big house, but I don't see how to get it."

"I know." He rubs his fingertips together. "We're lookin' at some serious scratch." He turns toward the door. "Let's go talk to the old gal and find out what she's up to."

Chapter 4

Katherine must've been watching for our return because she opens the door before we can knock. "Well, what do you think?" she asks as she leads us into the living room.

Ty and I perch on the edge of the sofa. "W-e-e-ll, holding a sale at the cottage is certainly no problem, but unfortunately, there's virtually nothing of value there," I begin.

Katherine offers a dreamy smile. "Jeff was utterly unmaterialistic."

That may be a very virtuous quality for humanity as a whole, but not if you're an estate sale organizer. Acquisitiveness is the name of our game. I try to be more direct to help Katherine understand the problem and prompt her to explain her proposal to divert profits from her sale into Mr. Singleterry's. "Much of the stuff in the cottage probably wouldn't sell. We'd end up hauling it to the dump eventually."

Katherine leans forward in her wheelchair and fixes her clear blue gaze on me. "But I want you to try to disperse Jeff's possessions to people who will appreciate them. It's what he would want. And your own website warns people not to discard anything before a sale because you never know what might sell."

Trapped by my own sales copy! I don't tell her that the warning is there to prevent people from "helping" us by discarding rare baseball cards and vintage Barbie dolls. It doesn't apply to dented aluminum frying pans and books covered in marginalia. I decide on a more indirect approach to get Mrs. Dupree to commit to letting Another Man's Treasure organize her sale. "It's true that we never know what might sell. Why don't you tell me a little more about Mr. Singleterry. Maybe that would help us...er...position his sale better."

"Jefferson Singleterry was a dear friend," Katherine explains. "He and my husband met in grade school, and they stayed friends throughout their lives, even though they took very different paths. Jeff was a brilliant man, but he lacked social skills. He had absolutely no ability to suffer fools. And he spoke his mind with brutal honesty."

"My kinda dude," Ty says.

"As the young people say, Jeff had no filters. Consequently, he was fired from a long string of teaching jobs. His wife left him and took their two kids. And finally, he washed up here. It was right around the time my multiple sclerosis got worse, and I started using a wheelchair. Gaston was concerned about leaving me alone here when he traveled for work, so he convinced Jeff to live in the cottage rent-free. Told Jeff he'd be doing us a huge favor to be here for me in case of an emergency. And so we lived very happily for over twenty years."

Katherine pivots her wheelchair so she can gaze at the spectacular show outside her window. "Last year, everything changed. Gaston was away at an architectural conference in London when I got the call that he'd collapsed and been taken to the hospital." She lifts her hands and lets them drop. "I've had medical problems for so long, I can hardly remember a time when I didn't require a doctor's care. But Gaston was the very picture of health. Seventy-two years old and took no prescription meds at all. Then one day..." She claps her hands sharply, making Ty and me both jump. "His aorta blew out. Abdominal aortic aneurism. He was dead before he reached the hospital."

She crumples into her wheelchair, shaken by the effort of telling her story.

"I'm so sorry for your loss." The phrase is a platitude, but what else can I say? I don't know her well enough for a hug, and honestly, she doesn't seem like she'd welcome even a hand-squeeze.

Ty and I exchange a glance. We've seen this scenario before—the healthier spouse dies first, leaving the weaker spouse behind with no protector. The silence stretches out and I feel I need to nudge her along. "And Mr. Singleterry...?"

"There was an enormous outpouring of sympathy after Gaston's death," Katherine continues. "My children, friends, colleagues—everyone gathered around for the memorial service and the tributes. But then..." She takes a deep, sorrowful breath. "...their lives had to move on, and I was left alone here. Alone except for Jeff. He was a tremendous support to me. He knew how to offer assistance without hovering or fussing. We ate breakfast together every morning and made a plan for the day."

She gazes into the distance. "And then, one morning he didn't come."

Katherine's lips set in a hard line.

Thank goodness Donna isn't here or she'd be bawling her eyes out. I feel a lump in my throat and notice Ty blinking as if he has sand in his eyes.

I'm curious how Jefferson Singleterry died, but I really don't need to know that, so I move on to the essential matter. "Can you explain a little more why you want us to divert some of the proceeds of your sale to Mr. Singleterry's heirs? He has so little of value. Won't the heirs be suspicious?"

Katherine offers a tired smile. "You haven't met Jeff's children. Matthew is rather like Jeff—smart, but antisocial. And Daphne is anxious and easily overwhelmed. Both of them have struggled to find their way in the world. They both need money, but they're proud. Giving them money by way of the estate sale would provide them with a way to accept the cash while saving face."

This makes sense, and now that I've seen Mrs. Dupree with her one-eyed feral cat and her dying houseplants, I don't suspect her of nefarious motivations. "Have his kids already taken the items they'd like to keep for sentimental reasons?" I ask. "We noticed there weren't many personal items."

"My daughter Celeste has asked them to empty out the cottage, but Matthew says it isn't his responsibility, and poor Daphne comes, breaks down in tears, and leaves. So holding this sale is the only way I can see to get the cottage emptied and ready for Isabelle to sell." She opens her pale blue eyes and again leans forward in her wheelchair. "Will you help me with my little deception?"

I glance around at the gorgeous art and one-of-a-kind furniture in Katherine Dupree's great room. This will be a six-figure sale. The cottage won't require much work. Why shouldn't I help poor Katherine out with her generous scheme?

"Sure, we can do it. How much money did you have in mind to give them?" I ask.

"Mmmm." She lifts one bony shoulder. "Maybe twenty thousand. Ten for each."

Ty fills his cheeks with air and blows it out. "Ain't no one going to believe the stuff in that house would sell for twenty grand." He snaps his fingers. "But how about this? We could say we found some cash hidden in the house. Believe me, that happens all the time, even with people who look like they were broke."

For the first time since we've been there, Katherine breaks into a smile that lights up her entire face. "Perfect!"

Ty has spontaneously come up with the perfect solution. I kinda wish we'd discussed this angle privately, but to retract the offer now would be like taking an ice cream cone away from a toddler. Not gonna happen.

We sign a contract and agree to start work on the dual sale next week.

On the way back to the office, I sit quietly gazing out the van window. I've fallen into the habit of always letting Ty drive because it gives me a few minutes of total downtime when I don't have to pay attention to children, house, husband, job, or traffic.

I need that break.

Mercifully, Ty's not the kind of person who feels the need to make chit-chat to fill a silence. He's absorbed in his own thoughts. But as he parks the van outside our office, I snap back to attention. "Do you think we're making a mistake with this cash transfer deception?"

Ty shrugs. "I was suspicious before we met her. But I feel okay about it now. Mrs. Dupree has had a lot of troubles in her life, but she doesn't complain. I admire that. She wants to help her friend's kids. No harm, no foul."

"Yeah." I unlock the office door. "Unless..." I turn to face Ty. "What if it's her own kids that she's trying to fool? Maybe they control her finances and won't let her give money to the Singleterrys." I plop into my desk chair. "I hate getting in the middle of family disputes."

Ty offers a short laugh. "Audge, by now you oughta know that's a cost of our business."

Chapter 5

We hear her before we see her.

"I'm b-a-a-a-ack!" Three days after we sign the contract for the Dupree sale, Donna sails through the office door with her arms outstretched.

I leap up from my desk. "We missed you so much! How was the trip?"

"Every day was so beautiful! I've been floating for two weeks."

Ty spots it before I do. "What's that big sparkler, girl?"

Donna looks down at her left hand. Then instead of holding it out for us to inspect, she hides it behind her back. "There's something I have to tell you."

"You're engaged. Congratulations. Audge and I figured he'd pop the question when you were over there."

Donna smiles but looks oddly nervous. "Yes, well...I'm actually more than engaged. Alex and I decided to go ahead and get married in Greece. We just had a little ceremony in the village church and had a party in the taverna afterward." Before Ty and I can say a word, Donna howls. "I'm so sorry you guys weren't there. You're the only two people I feel bad about leaving out."

"Man, I feel cheated." Ty puts on his best angry face. "I was countin' on a big blow-out with all-night dancing and lots of Italian and Greek food. I bought a new suit and everything."

"Oh my God, I'm so s-o-o-r-r-e-e-e!"

"He's teasing you, Donna. We're both delighted." I give her a big hug and Ty picks her up and spins her around.

"You double-crossed your mother, didn't you?" Ty asks with a grin.

"Our families are the reason we decided to get married in Greece. Since it's the second marriage for both of us, we wanted to keep it small. But my mother has never used the words 'small' and 'wedding' in the same sentence."

"How did she react when you told her the deed was done?"

"She cried for a solid hour and told me she'd never speak to me again. But she's called me three times this morning to ask about wedding gifts."

"So let's see the engagement ring," I demand.

Donna extends her hand to show off a large aquamarine stone surrounded by diamonds. A plain gold band sits under it. "It's the color of the Mediterranean," she sighs as Ty and I ooo and ah.

"You're gonna have a hard time gettin' your rubber gloves on over that," Ty says.

"Don't worry—I can always find a way to combine my two great passions: cleaning and jewelry." She gazes around the office which has grown dusty and cluttered in her absence. "What is that pile in the corner? And who left all this crap on my desk?"

"We haven't been able to find the packing tape dispenser since last week, so we're a little backed up on shipments," I explain.

While Donna dives into our mess, Ty and I fill her in on our new job at the Dupree house.

Donna's eyes widen as she attacks two weeks of accumulated mail on her desk. "This will be a social media bonanza! When can I start promoting it?"

"I'm going out there tomorrow to take some pictures of the best items so I can start doing pricing research and notify some of our best customers."

"Ooo—can I come with you?"

"I think not. Mrs. Dupree tires very easily and she asked me to come alone and only stay for an hour."

"All right. But make sure you take good photos. And take some of the house, too."

Chapter 6

Sean and I have decided to divide our family time into two chunks to accommodate his late-night shift patrolling the not-so-mean streets of Palmyrton. I take Wednesday morning off work, and we pile the kids in the car for a visit to New Jersey's own Turtleback Zoo. We're both subdued on the half-hour drive there, remembering less than thrilling class trips to the place from our own childhoods.

But from the moment we let the twins loose, they're thrilled with the outing. They squeal when they get to touch the sting rays in the water and watch intently to see which hole the prairie dogs will pop out of next. They don't mind that this zoo doesn't have polar bears and leopards—they have nothing to compare it to, so they're totally thrilled. We're the ones who wanted something glossier, but now we're glad to be in this smaller, more manageable venue.

Thea and Aiden are beside themselves with delight when we arrive at the spider monkey exhibit. Jumping up and down and pointing, Aiden keeps repeating a phrase that sounds like "curry gore."

"What's he saying?" I ask Sean.

"I don't know, but he's getting mad that we don't understand." He crouches down beside our son. "They're monkeys, buddy. Do you like them?"

"Curry g-o-o-re!" Aiden wails in frustration.

Thea points to a man in a University of Michigan cap. "Yewwow hat."

Finally, the ball drops. "Oh, Curious George and the man in the yellow hat! Yes, Aiden—these monkeys are just like Curious George."

Aiden smiles with satisfaction at being understood. Poor kid—it must be hard to have such dense parents.

We finally drag them away from the monkeys and stroll to the sea lions.

"They've really improved this place since we were kids," Sean says.

"I know. I remember a tiger pacing back and forth in a ten-foot cage. Even as a third-grader, I knew that was no way to treat such a magnificent wild cat."

I gaze off at a small herd of antelope. "Do you think the deer herd culling in Hamilton Park is a good idea?"

"In a balanced ecosystem, every animal has a predator to keep it from over-populating. The deer in New Jersey don't have any wolves to eat them. Their only enemies are cars."

"Yeah, I get that. But I'm not crazy about shooting in a place where there are so many hikers."

Sean rounds up the twins and straps them back in their double stroller. "Our hiking days are over until these guys can walk a couple miles under their own steam."

We arrive back home just in time for both the kids and Sean to crash into afternoon naps, giving me some free time to research the furniture I'll be selling at the Dupree estate sale. An hour quickly passes as I learn more about furniture designed in New York in the 60s and 70s.

When Sean comes downstairs from his nap, he's wearing a polo shirt, khakis, and a sports coat he only wears to work. With his short haircut and perpetually alert gaze, he looks like exactly what he is: a plainclothes cop. The revelers exiting Palmyrton's bars tonight will have to be pretty drunk not to spot Sean in their midst.

I put my arms around him and rest my cheek on his broad chest. "I wish you didn't have to go out there tonight."

"Me too." He kisses the top of my head. "Don't wait up."

As the mother of toddler twins, I'm not capable of keeping my eyes open past ten PM, no matter how much I'd like to try. I will sleep while Sean patrols the streets, but I know it won't be a deep, restful sleep. One part of my brain will be alert for the sound of his key in the lock, his step on the stairs.

Or worse, the late-night phone call no wife of a cop ever wants to receive.

I lift my head for a better kiss. "Be careful out there."

———————●———————

THAT NIGHT I DREAM of spider monkeys. For some reason, the monkey is ringing a bell. He rings it persistently, stops, then starts ringing it again. I reach out my hand to take the bell away and encounter a hard, thin object.

My phone.

It's ringing.

The screen announces it's Sean. Four in the morning! Why isn't he home?

"What's wrong? Where are you?" I demand without saying hello.

"Now don't freak out..."

There's nothing more likely to make me freak out than that warning. I bolt upright, wide awake, adrenaline surging. "What happened? Are you hurt?"

"I'm all right, but I won't be home for a while. I made an arrest."

I know that processing an arrest requires paperwork that will keep him at the station for a while. As my racing heart slows from a gallop to a canter, it dawns on me that he'd normally just send a text with his ETA, not call me before dawn. "What kind of arrest? Something serious?"

I hear him breathing.

"Sean?"

"Bill and I were patrolling the side streets off the green. The bars let out at two, and we strongly encouraged a few people to take Ubers home instead of driving. Things quieted down, and we were walking back to our car, ready to call it a night, when we saw these two guys a block away get into a scuffle." Sean pauses, and when he resumes, his voice sounds shaky. "It escalated from a shoving match to a fist fight in the time it took us to get to the corner. One guy slugged the other, and he went down hard. Then the guy who punched him took his wallet."

Sean falls silent except for his ragged breathing. Maybe I'm still groggy, but I don't understand the sense of dread hanging over our call. Sean's boss sent him out to watch for muggers and he interrupted a mugging. What am I missing? "So what happened? Is the victim okay? Did you catch the mugger?"

"I ran him down and made the arrest." Sean's voice cracks. "Audrey, it was my brother. It was Terry."

Chapter 7

Fallout from Terry's arrest blows through the Coughlin family like a tornado through a trailer park. The Coughlin sisters, Deirdre and Colleen, have already called in tears, demanding news. Naturally, Sean is not permitted to work on the investigation, so we actually get more information about what happened last night from Sean's oldest brother, Brendan. He's the sibling Terry called when he sobered up enough to realize he needed a lawyer.

Boy, does Terry need a lawyer!

Brendan sits at our kitchen table chugging black coffee and trying to talk to us while juggling multiple calls and texts.

Brendan glances at his phone screen. "The guy he hit was just released from the hospital. That's the only good news I've gotten since this mess started."

I attempt to get Brendan to start the story from the beginning. "What was Terry doing out drinking until closing time on a weeknight?"

"Had another big blow-up with his wife. Went out to drown his sorrows, I guess. And that's another thing. She's finally had enough. She filed for divorce today."

Can't say I blame her, but I keep that opinion to myself. Sean's parents, married over fifty years, will be shattered.

"So who was the guy Terry was with?" Sean asks.

"Some random drunk he met at the bar." Brendan drains his coffee mug in one go. "They were drinking together, and when the check arrived at closing time, there was some discussion about who owed what. They paid and walked out together but kept arguing about who owed who. Terry claims the other guy started the shoving match. Is that what you saw?" Brendan asks Sean, as his phone continues to buzz and chirp.

"I don't know. I was a block away," Sean wrings his hands. "I had no idea one of the guys was Terry."

Brendan holds up his hand for silence. "It's Mom. I better take this." He listens to a protracted monologue. "I'm doing my best, Ma. I think he'll be arraigned later today, and then hopefully they'll release him. No, Sean can't get them to drop the charges." Brendan listens again, rolling his eyes. "Ma, give it up. That's not gonna happen. I'll call you later. I got another call."

He ends that call and switches to another. "Hey, Charlie—I really appreciate you handling this on such short notice." He listens and nods. "Terry's had some DUIs, but no felonies. Whattya think? How bad is it? Yeah, okay."

Brendan pushes the phone away and shuts his eyes for a moment. When he opens them, he locks gazes with Sean. "Mom is freaking out. She thinks you should be able to fix this, like it's a parking ticket."

"He committed assault and robbery, Brendan!" Sean leaps from his chair. "He did it right in front of me and my partner. My partner had Terry cuffed before I even realized who we'd caught."

Brendan pats the air between them. "I know, I know. But try explaining that to Mom. For her, it's family above all."

"What about my family?" Sean shouts and waves his arm to encompass me and the kids. "I'm supposed to risk my career, my livelihood, to save Terry's sorry ass?"

"No, I get it," Brendan shifts uncomfortably in his chair. "But do you think you could do something to get the charges reduced? The lawyer thinks we could get him into a diversion program if it was just the assault. I mean, we could say self-defense on the punch. But the wallet..." Brendan massages his temples.

"What was he thinking? Why would he rob the guy?" I ask.

Brendan scowls. "Terry claims he paid more than his fair share of the bar bill. Said he was just taking what was owed to him. Mom believes him."

"Our mother is delusional," Sean shouts. "The wallet contained three hundred bucks in cash plus all the guy's cards, and Terry was running off with it. We recovered it from his pocket." Sean paces across the kitchen. "This rewriting history is the same crap he's been pulling since he was a kid. Always looking to blame someone else for his mistakes. Remember when—"

Brendan's phone rings again. "The lawyer," he mouths, cutting off Sean's tirade to take the call. "Three o'clock today for the arraignment. Should I be there? Okay, see you then."

Brendan rises to leave. "I know you're between a rock and a hard place." He claps Sean on the back. "Just see if there's anything you can do."

Brendan is out the door before Sean can respond.

My husband looks shell-shocked. "My family has lost their minds. All of them. Terry assaults and robs a guy, and somehow it's my fault for being there to see it happen."

I have absolutely nothing useful to say. My role here is to sit and listen while Sean works through his pain and anger. The Coughlins have always fought like cats and dogs among themselves, but whenever one of them is threatened by an outside entity, they circle the wagons. It seems my husband is not willing to play that game this time.

He paces a loop from the kitchen to the family room and back, gesturing at the silent monologue playing in his brain. Suddenly he stops and jabs his finger at me. "You know what, Audrey? Even if I could get Terry out of this, I wouldn't. The reason he's so irresponsible is because we've all been bailing him out of trouble his whole life. I started running interference for him in kindergarten. It's gotta stop."

I want to tell Sean it will all work out. But I don't believe it. There's a very real possibility that Terry Coughlin, son and nephew and brother of cops, will go to jail.

Chapter 8

After all the Coughlin drama yesterday, I'm really looking forward to escaping at work today. I'm due at the Dupree house at ten, which gives me time for a leisurely breakfast with the kids, and a relaxed drive across Palmyrton after rush hour has passed. I'm sailing along toward Hamilton Park daydreaming about a cute pair of shoes I saw advertised on Instagram when the car ahead of me slams on its brakes. Leaning on my horn, I manage to stop just before I rear-end him. And then I see the problem.

A deer stands on the left side of the road as three more leap from the forest's edge and follow her across. Yikes! I wave to the driver ahead of me to apologize for my rash horn-blowing, but I doubt he notices. We proceed slowly down the road toward the park. I'll be turning off soon for the Dupree house, so I stop daydreaming and focus on my driving. Before I reach the turn-off, the car ahead of me slows again.

More deer?

No, now there are people lined up across the road. People waving bright orange signs that picture a hunter with the "no" symbol drawn across him. They're shouting something I can't quite hear.

I roll down my window and get the sound track loud and clear. "Save our deer! No hunting here!" The leader approaches the car ahead of me with a clipboard, clearly wanting him to sign a petition. But the driver doesn't like being strongarmed into signing. He tries to inch forward, but the protesters won't budge. Will we be stuck here all morning?

Now the guy ahead of me honks his horn and makes a shooing motion.

Bad move. The protesters start thumping the hood of his car. The leader screams through a bullhorn urging his followers on. Geez, for supposed pacifists, these people are scary.

I'm about to call Sean to ask if the police are aware of what's going on here when I hear a siren in the distance. A minute later, two patrol cars roll up with lights flashing. The protestors stand defiant, but the cops are equally insistent. I watch as the cop tries to deescalate without success. Frustrated, he reaches for his handcuffs. Immediately, the other protesters whip out their phones and start recording.

Yeow! The new chief of police will love seeing this plastered all over social media.

The arrest tableau has drawn all the protesters to one side of the road, allowing the cars to edge by on the other.

As I make my escape, I lock gazes with one of the protesting women. Her curly hair whips in the breeze and her cheeks are rosy with the cold as if she were enjoying a fall outing. But the rage in her eyes tells a different story.

When I finally arrive at the Dupree house and ring the bell, the door is not opened by Katherine in her wheelchair, but rather by a tall, commanding woman with short gray hair and an angular face. She looks like a female version of Gaston Dupree, so I assume this is his and Katherine's daughter.

The woman looks me up and down as if she suspects me of being there to hawk vinyl siding.

"Hi, I'm Audrey Nealon, here to take some photos for the estate sale," I explain.

She opens the door wider. "My mother is resting. She's not having a good day, but she didn't want to cancel your visit." As I cross the threshold, she extends her hand and shakes mine with a fierce grip. "I'm Celeste Dupree. I'm visiting from California for a few days to work out some details of my mother's move to Shadow Glen."

Shadow Glen is the priciest assisted living community in the Palmyrton area, but I had assumed Katherine would be moving to a place close to one of her children. I guess my surprise must show because Celeste defensively adds, "I wanted Mother to come to a place near me in San Jose, but she doesn't want to leave her long-time doctor and her friends."

"I understand." I hope I haven't gotten this visit off on the wrong foot. "I won't be here long—just want to take some photos of the more unusual pieces so I can do some pricing research and notify some customers who might be interested."

Celeste follows me into the great room and peppers me with questions as I work. "How do you know that table is valuable? Who will you be sharing these photos with? What makes you think they'll be interested? Are you going to sell some things before the sale?"

As I patiently explain to her how I operate my business, she settles down. "How long have you been in this business?" she asks.

"Nearly twenty years. It started as a summer job when I was in college. But then I enjoyed it so much, I decided to make it my career and opened my own business a few years later." I crouch to get the correct angle on a photo of a large abstract sculpture. "How about you? What's your line of work?"

"I'm a software developer. My parents are—were—both artistic, but my brother and I are math/science types. Todd runs the IT department of an investment bank in Boston."

I smile at her. "You can be both. I was a math major in college."

This seems to impress her more than my estate sale organizing abilities. "You never considered a career in technology...finance...engineering?"

I laugh and shake my head. "Now you sound like my father. He was a math professor at Rutgers and for years he thought I was squandering my talent by running estate sales. But nothing you learn is ever wasted. I can add long columns of numbers in my head, and that skill comes in handy on sale days."

Celeste doesn't seem to realize I've made a little joke. "Your father disapproved of your career choice?"

I don't want to get into the long and complicated history of my parental relationships. "Yes, but that was a long time ago. He's gotten over it, and now he's proud of all I've achieved."

Celeste jams her hands into the pockets of her tailored black slacks and gazes out the window. "My father was a lion. He was strong, feared nothing, protected all of us. We thought of him as immortal. I know that sounds crazy, but we did."

She continues pacing across a geometric patterned rug. "He encouraged my brother and me to live our lives to the fullest and not accept any limitations. That's why I moved to California to work in high tech. That's why Todd stayed in Boston after he graduated from MIT. We both assumed my father would always be here to take care of my mother. My brother and I were stunned when Daddy died first."

She seems more outraged at the injustice of this than grief-stricken, so I see an opportunity to turn the conversation. "It must have been doubly shocking when Mr. Singleterry also died suddenly. What caused that?"

Celeste wrings her hands. "When Jeff failed to show up at Mom's house as usual and didn't answer his phone, she got a neighbor to check on him. He'd passed away in his sleep."

"Heart attack?" I ask as I move a lamp so I can get an unobstructed photo of a large expressionist painting.

Celeste shakes her head. "They did an autopsy and discovered the cause of death was renal failure. No one knows if he had a history of kidney problems because he staunchly refused to go to the doctor for anything. He was highly suspicious of what he referred to as the 'medical industrial complex.' He sometimes dosed himself with herbal remedies and supplements, so they speculated that something he took might have damaged his kidneys."

"How sad."

She flops down on the sofa, dangling one long leg over the other. "Foolish, really. Just because something is herbal doesn't mean it isn't dangerous. But no one could tell Jeff anything. Very opinionated."

Unlike you. "Yet he was devoted to your mother," I remind her.

She twists to give me a piercing look. "Mother says you plan to include the contents of the cottage in the sale. That's a waste of your time. We should just haul his stuff to the dump. I told Jeff's children that's what we'd do if they didn't take it themselves."

"And were you friends with his kids?"

She gives a dismissive snort. "Hardly. Even though Daddy and Jeff were the same age, Jeff got married much later in life, so his kids are fifteen to twenty years younger than Todd and me. Of course, I've met them, but I don't know them well."

Celeste jumps up again and follows me into the dining area. "I've gone through the cottage. Jeff's computer is worthless, and the furniture looks like it came from someone else's garage sale. You can't possibly get any money for that."

I can tell Celeste will never believe we raised twenty grand selling Singleterry's possessions. Good thing Ty came up with the hidden cash plan. Still, I need to appease her so we can go through the motions of holding the sale. "Oh, you'd be surprised at what will sell in an estate sale. For instance, some of his books might be valuable."

Celeste snatches an old book off a side table and waves it at me. "This is one of Jeff's books. He left it here the last time he visited my mother." She reads the title out loud. "*The Long Road to Salvation: the role of religious pilgrimages in medieval life*. Seriously? You can sell that?"

"Often, it's the obscure books that have the most value. Scarcity creates worth. There are ten million copies of *The DaVinci Code* floating around. Probably only one or two of that."

Celeste makes a pained face.

"Look, it's really no trouble for us to hold this small sale at the cottage during the big sale here. It won't slow us down. And it will make your mom happy. I think she'd be sad to see her old friend's possessions sent to the dump."

Celeste narrows her eyes. "Are you always so concerned about your clients' personal happiness?"

The more Celeste resists the idea of the small sale at the cottage, the more I lose my initial reluctance. "My work puts me in contact with lots of older people who are faced with giving up their independence and moving to assisted living. It's never easy. If you can do one small thing to make the experience less traumatic, I think you should do it."

"Fine. Fine!" Celeste pivots with a huff, tapping the smartwatch on her wrist. "I have errands to run. Just close the door behind you when you leave. It will lock automatically."

No sooner has Celeste banged out the front door than I hear a low electronic hum behind me, and Katherine rolls into the room.

"My daughter can be quite domineering. Thank you for standing up to her."

Chapter 9

That evening, my father and his wife Natalie come over for dinner. All the grandchildren on Sean's side of the family call his father Pop-Pop, leaving my father with exclusive rights to the name Grandpa, which Aiden and Thea currently pronounce as Gampa. Today, they have him hemmed in on the sofa as they scurry back and forth bringing him toys.

"Look, Gampa!" Thea drops a stuffed hippo in his lap.

"Tuck, Gampa!" Aiden runs over my father's feet with his favorite tractor-trailer.

"Read!" Thea demands, crawling onto his lap with a copy of *Sheep in a Jeep*.

I'm astonished by how well my reserved and cerebral father tolerates this. When I was a child, he had no patience for my silly toys. I figured he wouldn't play much with his grandchildren until they were old enough to learn chess.

But I was wrong. Dad makes the hippo dance with a giraffe. He crashes trucks complete with sound effects. And he reads the saga of the sheep and their traffic woes three times.

With the twins blessedly occupied, I retreat to the kitchen to enjoy the company of my stepmother as we prepare dinner. In quick succession we cover the health benefits of blueberries, the opening of a new Italian market, the closing of our favorite clothing boutique, and the controversy over the deer hunt.

"I had to swerve to avoid hitting a deer on my way home from yoga class last week," Natalie confides. "There really is a population crisis. Still, I don't like to think of the lovely creatures being shot."

"I had to drive past the protesters on my way out to my sale at the Dupree house," I tell Natalie as I search for broccoli that I'm sure is hiding in our over-stuffed fridge. "They're more than passionate about their cause. I'd say they're a little crazy."

The sudden silence from the family room causes me to glance up from my meal prep. My father sits on the sofa holding an open picture book in his hands, his mouth slightly ajar.

Puzzled, Aiden twists his head to look at his grandfather's face.

"Gampa, read more." Thea prods my father with both hands. Dad snaps back to attention, gives his head a shake, and resumes the saga of the bird who can't find its mother.

I shrug and return to chopping.

"Audrey, I want to show you how to prepare those herb plants in your garden for the winter," Natalie says.

Natalie knows that gardening falls into Sean's bailiwick, and I'm about to tell her to wait for his return when she shoots me a sharp look and jerks her head toward the backyard.

She wants to tell me something.

I follow her out to the patio where we feign interest in the oregano and rosemary. "I didn't want to worry you," Natalie begins.

Immediately, my stomach clenches.

"But your father has had a few...er...episodes lately, and I've persuaded him to get checked by his neurologist."

"What do you mean...episodes?"

"He blanks out for twenty to thirty seconds. Doesn't respond to my voice." She takes a deep breath. "I think he may be having mini strokes."

Chapter 10

On Thursday morning, Ty, Donna, and I arrive at Katherine Dupree's home to begin pricing and organizing for the sale. I've researched prices for all the most significant mid-century modern furniture and the artworks. I'll label them while Ty and Donna take care of the routine household items. For such a spacious home, there's actually not a lot of the small items that are time-consuming to price and sell. While we wait on the porch to be admitted, I give Ty and Donna a run-down. "The Duprees stopped entertaining after Katherine started using a wheelchair, and she seems to have been ruthless about purging items she no longer used. When I was here previously, I noticed that quite a few closets and cabinets are already empty. We should have no trouble getting the sale all set up by five today."

Mrs. Dupree lets us in. As in the past, she's stylishly dressed, but today she has a purse in her lap. "My friend is coming soon to take me out for the day." She smiles wanly. "I think it will be easier for all of us if I'm not here."

There's no arguing with that although agreeing wholeheartedly seems cruel. "Spending time with your friend will be a nice distraction."

Mrs. Dupree has marked a few items as Not For Sale—these pieces will be going with her to Shadow Glen on Friday. And there is a stack of moving boxes in the corner with her smaller possessions that are making the move. Everything else goes into the sale on Saturday.

I begin in the dining area with a large server featuring a dark green soapstone top and sleek burled maple drawers. Lovely, although large for most homes. But I think an interior designer I know might be interested. I price it at $4K. Opening the top drawer, I find an array of linens to remove and price. The next drawer also contains linens. The bottom drawer is empty except for a silver, tri-fold picture frame. I open it up to find three black and white photos that could be used to illustrate a Ralph Lauren ad. The first photo shows a young Katherine on a sailboat with Gaston. The wind lifts her pale hair as she extends one graceful arm toward her handsome husband standing behind the wheel. Truly a charmed life. The center photo shows a long-legged Katherine draped across a canvas beach chair with two children—presumably Celeste and Todd. The girl's face is solemn yet confident, her chin lifted in authority. The boy kneels in the sand, his hands on a bucket and spade. He appears to have looked up at the last moment to satisfy the photographer when he really would have preferred to continue his excavation. The third photo shows Katherine alone dressed in a stunning ball gown, her hair pinned in an elaborate up-do, glittering jewels at her ears and throat.

The photos are both fascinating and poignant, providing a glimpse of a more elegant, carefree era. To see Katherine so effortlessly beautiful a few years before her elegant body would betray her wrenches my heart. Of course, family mementoes like this will not go into the sale. Since Katherine hasn't departed yet, I go to ask her where she wants me to put this, so it doesn't get lost.

"I found these lovely photos in the server, Katherine. Where would you like me to put them?"

She barely glances at the photos before waving a dismissive hand. "Oh, those. You can throw them out. Sell the frame if you want."

"Throw them out!" I can't help disagreeing with her. "Oh, no—they're so beautiful."

Katherine shrugs. "No point living in the past."

"But your children would want them. Let's put them aside for Celeste and Todd," I suggest.

Katherine's eyes harden. She takes the frame from me, and with determined fingers opens the back, removes the photo of her and Gaston on the boat, and rips it in half.

Chastened by her irritation, I take the frame back. "I'll handle it, Mrs. Dupree."

The arrival of the friend who's taking her to lunch saves me from any more awkwardness. As the front door closes behind Katherine Dupree, I can't help but wonder if her husband was quite as devoted to her as I've been led to believe.

After finishing work in the great room, I bypass the kitchen where Donna is busy with dishes and housewares, and enter the master bedroom, which also faces the large rear terrace. It seems the Duprees still shared the room despite Mrs. Dupree's health problems. One side of the king-sized bed has ingeniously designed rails and handholds to make it easier for her to move from wheelchair to bed, and the huge master bath is barrier free. The walk-in closet holds a few items of Katherine Dupree's clothing that she's not taking with her, which I'll leave for Donna to handle. I focus on the furniture, books, and small artworks in the room.

After half an hour, I hear a tentative tapping sound and pause my work to listen. Nothing. I return to pricing and there it is again. Tap-tap-tap. Tap, tap.

I look around for the source of the sound. Could it be the cat? No, he's curled on a sunny window seat.

Surely, if someone were at the front door, they'd ring the doorbell. So when I hear the tapping again, I step through the sliding glass door onto the terrace to look around the back side of the house.

A thin woman with a cloud of frizzy brown hair stands with her face pressed against the door of Mrs. Dupree's study. She lifts her hand to knock again as I call out, "May I help you?"

The woman leaps as if electrocuted and turns to face me with wide eyes. "Who are you?" she gasps.

I smile and approach with my hand outstretched. "Hi, I'm Audrey Nealon. I'm working on organizing Mrs. Dupree's estate sale. And you are...?"

The woman backs slowly away. I feel like I'm a black bear and she's a startled hiker trying to remember the proper bear-encounter protocols. "I, I'm Daphne."

"Oh, Mr. Singleterry's daughter." I offer what I hope is a reassuring smile.

Her eyes get even wider. "How did you know that?"

"Mrs. Dupree mentioned you in connection with the cottage." I nod in the direction of the house her father once occupied. Something about Daphne seems oddly familiar to me, but I'm sure I've never met her before.

"Where is she?"

Daphne acts like I've got Katherine bound and gagged inside. But she's the one creeping around, peering through rear windows. I summon up the dignified authority of a British butler to reply. "Mrs. Dupree has gone out to lunch with a friend. She just left and won't be back for a while. Was she expecting you?"

Daphne shakes her head, making her mop of hair fly. "No, I wanted to talk to her again about my father's things." She sinks onto a patio chair, but the seat is damp from last night's rain, and she springs back up.

She's such a sad sack; I can't help feeling sorry for her. "I can let you into the cottage if you want to get some of your father's things. I believe Celeste told you that I'm going to be holding a sale there as well."

Daphne nods miserably. "I told her I needed some more time to find a truck...and maybe ask a friend if I could store some stuff in her basement...." She trails off, and I can see why Celeste is frustrated. Jeff passed away two months ago, and it's clear Daphne hasn't taken the slightest action toward clearing out his things.

"Mrs. Dupree is moving to assisted living at the end of the week." I state this fact and let Daphne draw her own conclusions. The time for negotiating has passed.

Daphne's big orphan eyes well with tears.

Oh, crap! I don't need this today. "But it's fine if you want to come right now to take some things away." I glance around. "Where's your car?"

"I left it in the Hamilton Park parking lot and walked through the woods to get here. My therapist says I need to spend time outdoors every day."

That's it! The other morning when I drove here and the road was blocked by the anti-hunting protesters, I think Daphne was in the crowd. But she was wearing a hat that day, so it's hard to be certain. I toss out a probe. "If you hike in the park regularly, you must have an opinion on the deer hunt."

Immediately, Daphne's forlorn expression dissipates, replaced by a fierce anger. "It's barbaric! The park rangers and hunters should be ashamed of themselves."

Hmmm—so it probably was Daphne out there on the protest line. "We-e-ell, I guess I could drive you back to your car if you want to get it and load it up." As soon as the words leave my mouth, I'm kicking myself for making the offer.

Daphne cocks her head as she considers, then shakes it no.

Whew!

"I don't really want much." Her voice is faint and tentative. "Maybe just one small memento."

Augh! This is heartbreaking. I keep my voice resolutely upbeat. "Sure, I'll unlock the door for you, and you can take what you want." Silently, Daphne follows me down the path toward the cottage. It dawns on me as I unlock the door that Jeff Singleterry obviously didn't share the key to his home with his kids, or Daphne wouldn't have been looking for Katherine earlier.

As I open the door and step back for her to enter, she releases a long sigh. Drifting through the room, running her fingers lightly across the back of the armchair and the keyboard of the computer, Daphne doesn't seem at all focused on finding a memento to take with her. I can see now why Katherine said Daphne was easily overwhelmed.

"How about a book?" I suggest. "Or there's a framed photo of your dad with the Duprees up in his bedroom."

Lost in her own thoughts, Daphne seems not to have heard me. "He never wanted to be a father," she says softly. "He wanted to be a monk."

A monk! A great battle sets itself up in my mind. Normally, I'm curious about people's lives and the unpredictable turns they take, but if I ask Daphne to elaborate, we might be here all afternoon. I have work to do.

"Did you visit him here often?" I ask instead.

"No, visiting him increased my anxiety. My therapist felt our contact was counterproductive."

Hmmm. And yet here you are, unable to come to terms with your father's death.

Daphne wanders over to the kitchen and gazes at the items on the shelves. She seems close to tears.

A long silence ensues. When I can no longer bear it, I announce, "I've got to get back to work, Daphne. You're welcome to stay here, and I'll come back later to lock up."

She jumps, surprised to find she's not alone. "Oh...oh, no, that's okay. I'll leave now." And she heads for the door empty-handed.

I'm about to say, "but you didn't take anything," however, my guardian angel stuffs a metaphysical sock in my mouth.

Daphne glides out of the house, wafting toward the woods like the fluff of a dandelion. As I watch her disappear, I notice a bright orange sign through the trees. Naturally, I have to wade into the woods to check it out.

Warning!

Bow Hunting in effect October 27 through November 30, excluding Sundays.

Stay on marked trails.

Chapter 11

I skitter out of the woods, looking over my shoulder. A pang of worry for Daphne strikes, but then I notice the wide trail just a few feet away. I guess she'll be okay—surely hunters would be out at dawn and dusk, not high noon.

As long as I'm down at the cottage, I might as well dive in to pricing here. I was almost done in Mrs. Dupree's bedroom when Daphne arrived. After texting Donna to let her know my whereabouts, I price the furniture in the living area in just a few minutes. The books will require a little more effort, so I leave them for now and head to the kitchen area of the first floor, where I find Jeff's collection of herbal supplements. Of course, these will have to be tossed, but I'm curious as to what he could have taken to bring on renal failure. I'm not one for herbal remedies myself, but as I prepare to drop the bottles into the trash, I realize I've seen these brands on the shelves at Whole Foods. None of it looks like something sketchy procured from a black-market herbalist.

"Hi there!"

I spin around to see a fiftyish man in the open doorway. He's all decked out in boots, hiking poles, a bright red fleece, and a hydration backpack like he stepped right out of an REI catalog.

"Are you holding an estate sale here?" he asks, taking a step over the threshold.

"Saturday," I say. "I'm just setting up today."

"Up at the big house, too?" His eyes gleam and he licks his lips like a ravenous tourist at a cruise buffet.

"Yes. We'll open at 8AM Saturday. No early birds." I come towards him to close the door.

Undeterred, he sticks his hand out to shake. "Bob Geary. I've been hiking past here for years. Stopped to talk to the old fella a few times. Jeff, his name was, right?" He stretches up on tiptoe to peer over my shoulder into the cottage. "Interesting man. Knew a lot about history. And herbs."

Not as much as he thought he did.

I'm not about to share Jefferson Singleterry's cause of death with this nosey parker, but I see an opportunity to get some information from him. I step out onto the cottage's small front porch to continue the conversation. "I was just disposing of his herbal remedy collection. It all looks like mainstream stuff. Did he know more than the average health food enthusiast?"

Bob nods his head vigorously. "Oh, yes. He was a specialist in medieval history, and he knew about all the herbs used by the monks and the nuns and the herbalists of that time. He even grew some stuff out there," he points to a weedy patch beside the cottage sectioned off with a border of rocks, "but I guess it's all dead now."

Maybe he grew the stuff that killed him. Somehow, that seems even worse than taking too much of something you bought. "Did he have particular ailments he was trying to cure?" I ask.

Bob gives a short bark of a laugh. "Now that's an interesting question. He looked very healthy to me, but It seems he started believing some of the weird stuff that people believed back in the Middle Ages. Like that illness was a punishment for your sins, and that your four humors are out of balance when you're sick."

"I've heard of the four humors. Let's see... phlegm, blood, and er..."

Bob helps me out. "Black bile and yellow bile. That belief persisted well beyond the Middle Ages. Jeff wasn't the only one who still followed it."

"And you?" I enquire. Bob is definitely the crunchy, granola-head type, but he appears pretty rational.

"Nah. I just enjoy talking to people about their passions. I stopped to chat with Jeff one day when he was out in his garden, and before long, he was telling me all about medieval healers and the scourges they tried to cure."

Bob lowers his voice even though there's no one around to overhear us. "He was preoccupied with his urine."

I wrinkle my nose. "Urine?"

"Apparently that's the first thing medieval medical practitioners checked when they were treating a patient." Bob chuckles. "Jeff loaned me a book about it. There were these old drawings of a doctor holding up a flask of piss next to the bedridden patient."

Hmmm. Maybe that's why he was taking herbs that affected his kidneys. Jeff Singleterry gets odder and odder the more I learn about him.

"It took me a while to read the book—not exactly a Tom Clancy novel—and then on the day I was bringing it back, I got over here and the place was surrounded by EMTs and cops," Bob explains. "I asked what happened, but they wouldn't tell me. Since I never saw Jeff again, I figured he must have died."

He lifts his eyebrows at me, waiting for confirmation.

"Yes, he passed away in his sleep. And Mrs. Dupree, in the big house, is moving to assisted living."

"She was Jeff's friend with all the afflictions, right?"

"Afflictions? That's a strange word." I feel compelled to speak up for Katherine Dupree. She's a strong woman and she doesn't perceive herself as afflicted. "She uses a wheelchair, that's all, and Jeff used to help her out."

"Uh-huh," Bob says, in the tone of someone humoring the misguided.

Normally, I'm quite good at shutting down an unwanted conversation, but there's something weirdly addictive about talking to Bob Geary. He keeps leading me into deeper water. "Why did Jeff consider her *afflicted*?"

"He said it was her destiny to suffer."

I step away from him. "That's awful. No one is born to suffer."

Bob lifts his hands to the cloudless sky. "Just reporting what Jeff used to say. I still have his book. You want me to return it so you can sell it?"

I turn to go into the house. "That won't be necessary. Just keep it as a memento."

"I don't mind. I could—"

I see salvation coming down the garden pathway in the form of Ty carrying a box of supplies. Ty looms over Bob and gives him the prison death stare. "No early birds."

"Okay...sure. I'll come back on Saturday." Bob waves and lopes back into the woods.

Ty turns his glare on me. "What's wrong witchu? You down here all alone with some strange dude."

"Oh, he was harmless."

I think.

But I'm kinda glad Ty got rid of him.

Chapter 12

Now that Ty is here, I'm free to focus on the books while he handles pricing the rest of the items. My preliminary scan of the shelves reveals that the books are all nonfiction. Even Chaucer must've been too entertaining for Jefferson Singleterry. I'm always fascinated by the way people organize—or don't organize—their books. Some people arrange by size and color, which makes me suspect they're more concerned with appearances than with reading. Others just toss the books on the shelves wherever they fit. And there are folks like Mr. Singleterry, with their own personal Dewey Decimal system. I find a tattered index card taped to a middle shelf. It contains a diagram of the shelves and the subjects of the books to be found there. The categories include, "Lives of the Saints," "Monastic Life", "Pilgrims and Pilgrimages," "Illness and Suffering," and "Herbs and Healers." I can't help smiling—it's like medieval *Jeopardy. I'll take Pilgrims for five hundred, Alex.*

Almost all the books were published by small academic presses, which means they had very small print runs. Scarcity could make some of them valuable although not at the stratospheric levels reserved for first editions of beloved books. But when I open a few books at random, I see that Jeff has underlined passages in pencil and written marginal notes on virtually every page in tiny, crabbed writing.

That means my go-to used book dealer will probably reject all these. I take pictures of some of the spines so I can double-check with him. However, I'm pretty much resigned to selling them for a buck a piece at the sale.

One book catches my eye: *The Healer's Art: Herbs, Incisions, and Intercessions.*

I set down the book and walk over to the kitchen shelves to point out the herbal supplements to Ty. "That guy Bob said Jeff was an herbalist and grew some of his own herbs." I open a bottle of Echinacea half expecting to find dried petals inside, but it contains mass-produced capsules. "I wonder if the stuff in these bottles killed him, or if it was something from his garden?"

Ty arches his eyebrows. "And that matters, why?"

"You know me, perennially curious." I take out my phone and snap a picture of the herb bottles on the shelf. "Okay—get rid of them."

Between the herbs, the expired food in the pantry, and the tattered sheets and towels, Ty soon has a big black bag to haul out to Mrs. Dupree's garbage can. When he reenters the house, he's not alone.

And he's not happy.

Given Ty's hardcore aversion to early birds, I figure this guy must have some compelling story or Ty wouldn't have let him get this far.

"Audge, this is Matthew Singleterry."

Ah! That explains it.

I'd never guess that Matthew and Daphne are twins. Not only do they not look alike, but they also don't even seem to be the same age. Matthew looks simultaneously young and old. He has a round baby-face, but his hair is thinning. He carries himself in the awkward manner of a recent grad who hasn't been out in the working world for long, but he has the wide, podgy middle of a soccer dad. He's wearing a tee shirt promoting a video game that Sean's middle-school nephews play, and the kind of baggy gray work pants that Donna's grandpa dons to tend his tomato patch.

Most of all, he has a chip on his shoulder that would require a crane to remove.

"What gives you the right to set a price for my dad's stuff?" he asks as he trails me around the cottage while I price things.

I pause with a five-dollar sticker poised above a table lamp. "I price things based on my experience of what the market will bear." I adhere the tag, talking as I move to the next item. "You're free to take any of this, Matthew. It belongs to you and your sister. She was here earlier today, but she didn't take anything."

"What would I want with this old junk?" he snaps. "Besides, I have no place to put it. I share a rental house, and I have to keep all my stuff in my bedroom."

So why complain about me?

Unintimidated by Ty's simmering glower, Matthew persists in questioning me. "What will you do with the stuff that doesn't sell?"

"Donate it to charity or, as a last resort, take it to the dump. We try to keep as much stuff out of the waste stream as possible, so we prioritize donating or recycling." I've reached Jeff Singleterry's vintage desktop computer. "Do you know if your father kept any financial records on here? Any private information you might want to erase before we sell it?"

Matthew blows out a dismissive huff of air. "My father didn't believe in online banking. He got his Social Security checks delivered by snail mail. He filed his income tax with a pen and a paper form. He probably has his money buried in coffee cans out in the woods."

I file this detail away. It will come in handy when we "discover" the cash Katherine wants to give to Matthew and his sister.

Matthew lifts and drops one end of the keyboard after I put a $25 price-tag on the hard drive. "No one will buy this relic."

"Never say never," I respond breezily. "Sometimes computer geeks show up and buy old models for the parts. If it doesn't sell, we'll take it to electronics recycling."

Matthew frowns at the computer monitor's dark screen. "My father only got this because the obscure historical journals he submitted papers to finally refused to accept his typewritten manuscripts. It's not even connected to the internet."

Now that he mentions it, I can see there's no modem or router. "How did he submit the manuscripts with no email?" I ask.

"My sister would do it for him. Or Katherine Dupree. One of them would come over and put the document on a flash drive and take it to their own computer to send off." Matthew throws back his head. "I refused to indulge his ridiculous Luddite behavior."

Of course, you're too good for that.

"I take it from the books on the shelves here that your father was a scholar of medieval history?"

"Medieval *religious* history," Matthew clarifies. "Such a booming field."

I think of the crucifix upstairs and Daphne's assertion that her father longed to be a monk. "Was your father a practicing Catholic?"

"Not since they stopped saying mass in Latin in the early sixties. He was not a fan of mass on Saturday and folk songs." Matthew sways and strums an imaginary guitar. "But it worked out well for me and my sister. At least we didn't have to go to school with the nuns the way he did."

"And what's your line of work?" I enquire. Given that he's hanging around here in the middle of a workday, he's clearly no corporate wheeler-dealer.

"I'm, uh, between gigs at the moment. I'm a consultant to video game developers."

Someone who plays video games for a living is making fun of someone who studies thousand-year-old history for a living. Pot, meet kettle.

I'm getting tired of this man's company and it's close enough to five to call it a day. "Well, Matthew, I'm going to be locking up here in a moment. I'll finish the pricing tomorrow. It's been nice meeting you, and as I said, feel free to take anything with you that you don't want to go into the sale."

Matthew jams his hands in his pockets and heads for the door. Before exiting, he looks back at his father's home. "Sixty-five years of devotion to the Duprees and this is how it ends. What a total waste."

TY MUTTERS SOME CHOICE curses under his breath as Matthew rattles away in his broken- down Ford. "Don't see why Mrs. Dupree wants to give any money to *him*. Nasty!"

"I agree. His sister's not much better. Not cranky, but not very appealing. Neither one of them had a good relationship with their father, so I don't understand Mrs. Dupree's concern for them. But it's her money." I look around. "Where do you think we should say we found the stash?"

Ty scratches his head. "There's no basement or attic. And with Matthew showing up when we're practically done here, it's hard to claim we found it in a cabinet or closet." He moves the dingy kitchen curtain to one side. "What's that statue out in the garden? We could say we decided to move it onto the porch and found something underneath."

We troop out to the patch of soil outlined by rocks that once was Jeff Singleterry's herb garden. Most of the plants are dead and dry now, except for one that resembles the rosemary plant Sean grows in a big pot by our back door. In the middle of the plot stands a small statue of a man dressed in long robes with his hand outstretched. A stone bird sits on his shoulder, while another eats from his hand.

"Must be Saint Francis," I say. "Wasn't he the patron saint of animals?"

"Beats me," Ty says. "But little garden statues like this sell pretty well, so I think we really should move it up onto the porch and price it." He rocks it back and forth to ease it out of the ground. "Not that heavy—must be hollow inside."

Ty lifts the statue and I look into its base. "Yep, there's a good-sized space. I think we could definitely claim we found cash stuffed in there."

Ty carries St. Francis to the porch and sticks a $20 price tag on him. "Problem solved."

Chapter 13

I arrive home long before Sean to squeals of delight from the twins. As I pull them into my arms and inhale their sweet aroma of baby shampoo and apple juice and Cheerios, I can't help thinking about the other twins I met today. Yes, Matthew and Daphne Singleterry were once adorable little toddlers full of love and joy.

Their mother once had limitless dreams for them. And their father...well, apparently he was never charmed by the new lives he helped create.

Roseline interrupts my musings with her daily factual update on who ate, who napped, and who pooped. After she leaves, Thea and Aiden pull me into their games. As I help them toss Nerf balls through a hoop and build a tower with blocks, my thoughts drift back to the final half-hour I spent at the Dupree house.

After Ty and I walked back to the main house from the cottage, we encountered Mrs. Dupree as she returned from her outing with her friend. She gulped and closed her eyes for a long moment when she saw the price tags affixed to all her precious possessions. I worried we might be greeted with tears, but she maintained her composure. And when we told her about the hollow St. Francis statue as our proposed repository for the faux stash of cash, she was delighted. Even after I told her that both Singleterry kids had dropped by and had not been particularly friendly, she was unfazed.

Her plan is to tell Jeff's kids after the sale is over on Saturday that we found the cash and invite them to her new residence at Shadow Glen to receive the money after Celeste goes back to California on Tuesday. The situation still seems dicey to me, especially now that I've met the weird recipients of Mrs. Dupree's generosity, but the wheels have been set in motion and I have to roll with it.

Just as the kids are losing interest in building and knocking down towers, Sean calls to tell me he's hung up at work. More complications stemming from Terry's arrest. The ingredients for dinner are in the fridge, and the recipe is in his file box of favorites. Can I get dinner started?

I agree—what choice do I have if we're ever going to eat tonight? I hate cooking from his recipe cards because I know there are all kinds of secret substitutions and adjustments he pulls out of his head when he cooks his favorites. I, on the other hand, follow the directions slavishly and the dish inevitably turns out wrong.

I try to get the twins interested in a new game that doesn't produce a huge mess or cause mortal injury so I can focus on cooking. We settle on "shopping" which involves pushing their toy carts around the family room and loading them up with anything that isn't nailed down.

While I'm chopping ingredients for dinner, my phone buzzes with two calls from prospective clients. I collect contact info from them and send them links to our website as I steer the dog away from a chunk of onion that's hit the floor.

"Mama, come play!"

"Okay—in a minute." I keep chopping even as my phone lights up with text messages from customers with questions about items in the Dupree sale. Donna's social media announcements have done their work.

"Mama, look at Aiden."

I stare at my phone. Two competing art dealers are interested in one of the paintings from the Dupree home. Ka-ching! "Yes, very nice," I call into the family room without lifting my gaze from the screen.

I hear a crash, a split second of dead silence, an ear-splitting howl.

I run into the family room to find Aiden flat on his back with a lamp on top of him. A bump rises on his forehead and a small trickle of blood runs toward his eye.

Thea, frightened by the volume of her brother's shrieks, begins to cry as well.

I cradle my son in my arms. How could I have let this happen? That stupid phone is a never-ending connection to work. I need to put it down and focus on my family life when I'm at home.

Eight hours a day should be enough for work.

Except it never is. Not when I'm responsible not only for my own livelihood, but also for that of Ty and Donna.

Aiden soon forgets about his tangle with the floor lamp. But I don't. I power down my phone and set it out of the way in the dining room to charge.

I won't look at it again until the morning.

Chapter 14

The Saturday of the Dupree sale dawns sunny and crisp—a perfect fall day. Cars are parked all along the road leading to the house, and an orderly line of customers snakes down the driveway. Ty, Donna, and I march past our future customers, and Donna promises she'll return shortly to pass out numbers.

Since Mrs. Dupree has made her move to Shadow Glen, I now have the key to the house. As soon as I open the door and walk in, I feel her absence. The house has lost its animating force; now it's just four walls filled with some very nice furniture and art.

No need to get morose. I shake off my feelings and kick into high gear. A lot of high-ticket items and very few odds and ends means a profitable sale with less menial work for us. Some of the folks outside have come simply to get a glimpse of this architectural gem and may leave empty-handed. But I've had enough messages from dealers, designers, and collectors to be confident we'll sell most of the house's contents.

The simultaneous sale at Jeff Singleterry's cottage means that Ty must manage that on his own, while I've hired his friend Lamar to help with any heavy lifting—or unruly customers—at the main house. Before departing for the cottage, Ty gives Lamar his orders. "You do everything Audge and Donna tell you. Carry the heavy stuff out for folks. And when you're not busy with that, keep your eyes open for people tryin' to boost the small items, hear?"

Lamar agrees. He's even bigger than Ty, but so sweet and amiable it's hard to imagine any potential shoplifters will be intimidated by him. I send Ty off with assurances that Donna and I will be fine at the big house, and five minutes later, we open the doors.

A horde of shoppers swarms in. Despite the size of the house and the open floorplan, there's a traffic jam because each and every person pauses before the huge windows to admire the view of the stunning fall foliage outside.

"Wow! If I lived here, I'd never move."

"Imagine waking up to that view every day."

"Never mind the furniture. I want to buy that view!"

And from our youngest customer, a little boy accompanying his mother, "I wanna go out there!"

But the truly serious shoppers know exactly what they want. They shoulder past the looky-lous and examine the pieces they came here to buy. Since all the Duprees' furniture is in excellent condition, I'm soon accepting payments and sending Lamar off to load purchases.

"This is great!" Donna says at midmorning. "We've made as much money in two hours as we usually make in a day, and I haven't had to do more than wrap up a few bowls.

No sooner have the words left her mouth than we hear a woman shout, "No, Saxon!" followed by the sound of shattering glass. Since Donna is finishing a transaction, I go off to investigate.

In the kitchen I find a Millennial mom dressed head-to-toe in Lululemon yoga gear and carrying a designer thermal mug that probably cost more than my entire set of kitchen dishes. Her son—perhaps eight or nine—is surrounded by a pile of glass shards and a crowd of horrified onlookers.

"That child pulled over a stunning crystal pitcher," a pursy-lipped older woman reports.

The kid begins to wail although he's clearly unhurt.

"It shouldn't have been left on the edge of the counter," the mother snaps.

Although the pitcher had nice, clean lines, it wasn't crystal. I'd priced it at twenty-five dollars, and although Ty would undoubtedly have demanded payment on the basis of "you break it, you bought it," I decide against arguing with Millennial Mom. She looks like trouble. Grabbing a broom, I sweep a path for the kid to return to his mother's side. "Please hold his hand while you finish your shopping," I say with a tight smile.

"Come on, Saxon," the mother extends her hand.

"Noooo! I'm too big to hold hands." He heads to the kitchen sliders and runs outside with Millennial Mom in hot pursuit.

Good—they're headed to the cottage. Ty will settle that brat down with one look.

Returning to the check-out table, I find Donna talking to a tall, wiry man. When he turns to face me, I nearly keel over. It's Gaston Dupree, looking like he just stepped off the sailboat in the photo Katherine tore in half.

"Audrey, this is Todd Dupree," Donna says. "Mrs. Dupree's son."

"Wow, you really look like your father," I say, regaining my composure. "The resemblance is uncanny."

The expression on his face indicates he's heard this countless times and is sick of it. "I came down from Boston for the day to see what's going on here." His words are directed at me, but his gaze is fixed over my left shoulder. He doesn't have the commanding presence of his father. Instead, he seems rather awkward and pugnacious. I don't know why he's acting like the sale is a surprise to him.

"I run Another Man's Treasure Estate Sales. Your mom hired me to clear out the house so she can put it on the market." I keep my voice pleasant and neutral.

Todd flinches as if my statement carried a slight electric charge. "As usual, my sister has taken charge and strong-armed my mother into following her plan."

Whoa! How am I supposed to respond to that? I decide a simple statement of fact is the best approach. "Your mom hired us to run the sale two weeks ago."

"But I only found out about it two days ago," Todd snaps.

I think about the blank spots in the house where items had clearly been removed before Katherine Dupree ever met me. I assumed both kids had taken the items they wanted to keep after Katherine made the decision to move. Did Celeste cut her brother out of the opportunity to keep some family heirlooms?

I stare blankly at Todd, not sure what else I can possibly say. He pivots away from me, jamming his hands in the pockets of his fleece jacket as he stares at the crowd of shoppers picking through his family home. Always a traumatic sight, which is why we recommend that relatives stay away on the day of a sale.

While Todd watches, a woman lifts a large ceramic bowl with a swirling green and gold glaze, examining it from one angle and another. Finally, she sets it back down, at which point another woman moves in and snatches it up.

Todd emits a scornful laugh. "Hope she enjoys that more than my mother did. It was made by one of my father's girlfriends." Todd points across the room. "That folding screen was designed by another. Life was so cozy here surrounded by my father's trophies."

Yikes!

Donna shoots me a look and slithers away. "Let me help you with that!" she calls to a customer who's carrying a small chair with no difficulty whatsoever.

Todd looks down at his high-end running shoes and scuffs the floor like an awkward teenager. "Sorry for being an ass," he mutters.

A wave of sympathy washes over me. Families are so complicated! No wonder Todd didn't want to take any mementoes from the house. "Can I get you anything?"

Todd blows out a breath. "Nah. I see you've already sold the cabinet where Dad used to store the forty-year-old scotch." He keeps talking without making eye contact. "My sister says I throw myself into my work when I can't deal with emotional problems. I'm struggling with my mom needing to move to assisted living. Guess I thought if I ignored the problem, it would go away." He looks up and meets my gaze. "Celeste tackles every problem head-on."

I smile. "I imagine she does."

"When she told me the house was going on the market on Monday, I couldn't get my head around it. I had to see it with my own eyes to make it real."

"I understand. Why don't you walk around and say your goodbyes," I suggest.

Todd nods and slouches off, muttering something under his breath that I don't catch.

Later in the afternoon, Millennial Mom reappears with her bratty son, looking madder than a Starbucks barista who's run out of oat milk. "Look at what Saxon picked up out in the garden!"

I sincerely hope the kid hasn't brought a handful of deer droppings into the house.

But what my outraged customer shows me is much worse: a long metal arrow with a viciously pointed tip, stained brownish red.

I recoil as she waves it under my nose. "He picked it up outside that little cottage. He could've been seriously hurt. Thank God, I got it away from him."

Saxon gazes at the arrow longingly, making me suspect his mother had to pin the kid down to pry that arrow out of his grubby, violence-loving fingers.

I plaster a look of concern on my face. "So sorry that your son stumbled over this. There's bow hunting for deer going on in the park at certain times of the day this autumn. I guess the arrow wound up over here because of that."

I hold out my hand to take the arrow and Saxon shrieks and falls to his knees. "No! It's mine! I found it!"

His mother's eyes widen in horror. "Hunting! I would never have brought my child here if I had known I was putting him in the line of fire of hunters!"

"I don't think—"

"I'm never coming to one of your sales again." She grabs Saxon's arm and hauls the screaming kid away.

After that little dust-up, the final two hours of the sale fly by. When we shoo out the last customers and lock the front door, the Dupree house is practically empty.

"Just two end tables left in the back bedrooms," Donna reports. "One of them had some sports trophies inside—looked like they might have been from summer camp. Do you think the Dupree family might want them?"

Given how Mrs. Dupree reacted when I urged her to keep those framed photos, I'm pretty confident that the family doesn't want to keep anything else from the house. "No, I think you can toss those," I tell Donna.

"And there's this weird carving." Donna eyes an abstract ebony figure. "I wonder if another girlfriend of Gaston's made this."

I glance over my shoulder. "That reminds me—did you ever see Todd leave?"

"No, but he might've gone out the back. We left the sliders open so people could get down to the cottage."

At that moment, Ty arrives. "All done down there. I sold St. Francis, but not that old computer. And there are some books left to dispose of." He looks around the empty great room in the main house and whistles. "Man, everything's gone. How much did we make?"

I slide toward him a sheet of paper with the final tally written down. I feel that saying the impressive number aloud will make the money—earned with so little effort—go up in a whiff of smoke.

"Wow! We ridin' high today!" Ty twirls Donna around in an impromptu dance.

"I'll take a check over to Mrs. Dupree on Monday," I say as we lock up the house and prepare to leave. "And she can tell Matthew and Daphne whatever story she wants about the money we *found* "—I wink and elbow Ty—"in the garden statue."

Chapter 15

I find I've been happier since limiting my screen time to certain hours of the day. My free time feels truly free, and once I've broken the habit of automatically checking my phone every few minutes when I'm at home, I discover myself going for hours without looking at the thing. I never miss anything related to work that can't easily be dealt with the next day, and I'm a lot more peaceful not knowing about the latest shootings, bombing, and invasions going on across the globe.

Thus it's not until I sit at my desk on Monday morning that I see the headline from *Palmyrton Now!*, our local news website. "Police Investigate Death of Hiker Shot by Arrow in Hamilton Park."

I feel a stab of guilt for making fun of Millennial Mom's dramatic fear of hunting-related injury. "Donna—look at this," I call out. "Someone was actually killed by a bow hunter."

"Yeah, it was on the Jersey news last night. They didn't say his name, or exactly where in the park it happened. But apparently he'd been lying out there for a while before they found him." Donna shivers. "He might've been shot on Saturday when we were busy with the sale. Maybe the arrow that kid found was shot by the same hunter."

I search online for more news on the incident and come across an article in which the deer hunt protesters are interviewed. "This tragedy was inevitable," a quote from the leader reads. "New Jersey is not Wyoming. The park never should've allowed this hunt in such a populated area. Now, they'll shut the hunt down, but it's too late for the victim."

A diabolical thought pops into my head. "Donna, do you think the anti-hunt protesters could've done this in order to shut down the hunt?"

"Kill an innocent man in order to save the deer from dying? Geez, that would be extreme!"

"Sean will know something." I text my husband at work, then try to focus on other matters while I wait for him to reply. Half an hour later, I get a message:

Long, complicated story. Will discuss tonite.

Ugh. I hate waiting, but Sean hates typing long text messages and he can't call me with details of an active investigation.

I reply: *Just tell me this. Did it happen anywhere near the border with the Dupree property?*

Yes.

⊷◉⊶

AFTER LUNCH, I'M SCHEDULED to visit Katherine Dupree at Shadow Glen to deliver the proceeds of the sale. At her request, I've cut three checks—two made out to the Singleterry children for ten thousand each, and one to Mrs. Dupree for the balance of the proceeds. As I slide them into an envelope, I feel a final twinge of misgiving, but it's too late to change course now. I head out for Shadow Glen.

I've often driven past the stone columns marking the driveway and the sweeping, manicured lawns, but this will be my first visit inside. The central part of the building was once a stately mansion. Artistically designed wings have been added to provide modern accommodations for elderly people who need assistance with daily living. The front door looks like the entrance to a lovely home, but it's locked and monitored by a security camera and a buzzer. I announce that I'm Audrey Nealon here to visit Mrs. Dupree, and after a brief wait, the door unlocks.

A nicely dressed woman greets me from behind a polished mahogany desk in the foyer. While smiling cordially, she asks to see my ID, checks a list, and finally summons someone to escort me to Mrs. Dupree.

The setting sure is elegant, but the security rivals that at the county jail. We pass an arts and crafts room, a game room, and an exercise room before arriving at a small sitting room where Mrs. Dupree awaits me in her wheelchair.

"Here's your visitor, Mrs. Dupree," the aide announces brightly. "If you need anything, just ring your buzzer."

A pendant with an electronic call button now hangs around Mrs. Dupree's neck. She makes a pained face at the aide. "I'll be fine, thank you."

My first impression is that Katherine Dupree seems to have shrunk in the days since I last saw her in her home. Her previous energy has been replaced by a listless acceptance of her fate.

I don't bother asking how she is. "Hi, Katherine. The sale was very successful. Just about everything sold." I hand her the envelope. "Here are the checks, made out just as you requested."

When she pulls the checks from the envelope and sees the two made out to Matthew and Daphne, her face lights up. Katherine raises her gaze to me. "Thank you, Audrey. You have no idea how much this means to me. I can finally right some old wrongs."

I'm not sure how I'm expected to respond to this cryptic statement, so I change the subject. "We sold almost everything from Jeff's cottage except his old clunker computer and some books. We'll donate the books and recycle the computer. Matthew said there were no financial records stored on it."

Katherine offers me a wistful smile. "No, Jeff only used it to write his academic articles. Gaston mocked him for resisting modern technology so insistently." Her expression hardens. "Of course, Gaston mocked anyone who didn't see the world his way."

Another crack appears in the rock that was Gaston Dupree. "How did you and Gaston meet?" I ask since Katherine seems to want to chat.

Her gaze drifts to a faraway time. "My parents sent me to Barnard College ostensibly to study art, but really so I'd meet a nice young man at Columbia who would go on to become a doctor or a lawyer or a stockbroker and provide me with the same kind of quiet, privileged life my father had provided for my mother in suburban Connecticut. Instead, I slipped out from the watchful eye of my dorm house mother, violated curfew, and rode the subway down to Greenwich Village. I heard Allen Ginsberg reading poetry at the San Remo Cafe and listened to Miles Davis playing trumpet at the Blue Note."

"Sounds like fun," I say.

"Katherine smiles a dreamy smile. "And I met Gaston. He'd come to New York from Rhode Island. When I met him, he'd been out of architecture school for a year and had already quit his entry-level job at a prestigious firm and waltzed off with one of their most prominent clients. He was audacious! I dropped out of college to follow him to Paris. We married over there. My parents were horrified."

"Very romantic," I reply.

Her face grows solemn. "Neither of my parents lived to see Gaston achieve financial success. They died worrying that I'd be left penniless. As it turned out, money was the least of our troubles."

Is she referring to her illness? Or maybe she considers Gaston's infidelity the worst of their problems, but of course Katherine doesn't know I know about that. I've chosen not to mention that Todd came to the sale claiming he didn't know what was going on.

"And when did you meet Jeff?" I ask. "Was he in New York City when you were in college?"

"Yes. He'd left the monastery by then and had started grad school in history at Fordham University. Gaston and I saw him occasionally. But it wasn't until we'd moved to the house in Palmyrton, and Jeff was teaching in New Jersey, that he and I became friends." She sinks into silence for a bit, then resumes. "I cherished Jeff's friendship, but it wasn't—"

"Oh, there you are, Mrs. Dupree!" A young nurse pops into the sitting room. "I've been searching all over. It's time for your meds."

At first, Katherine looks irritated by the chirpy young woman's interruption. Then her expression changes, and she pivots her wheelchair toward the door. "Thank you for visiting with me, Audrey. I appreciate all that you've done."

As I watch Katherine Dupree's wheelchair rolling away, I wonder what else she was about to say regarding her and Jeff's friendship.

I suppose I'll never know.

Chapter 16

As soon as Sean arrives home that night, I start pumping him for details about the hunting death. "Could it have happened on Saturday?" I ask as I strap the twins into their highchairs. "Because one of our customers found an arrow out in the garden behind Mr. Singleterry's cottage. And it looked like it had blood on the tip."

Sean shows an immediate interest. "What did you do with it?"

"Threw it away during the post-sale clean-up."

Sean throws up his hands. "Damn! That could've been important evidence."

"How was I to know?" I dole out cubes of sweet potatoes on the kids' trays. "But you know, the garbage is probably still out there in the cans. There are a lot of bags, but nothing gross or rotten."

Sean reaches for his phone. "I'll send some techs out there to search for it."

I wait until Sean is finished with his call and the kids have moved on to cubes of chicken. "Since I was so helpful, maybe you could tell me more about what happened to the victim."

"You're relentless, Audrey. That's what I love about you." He pats my hand. "The pathology report says the time of death was sometime between noon and five on Saturday."

I shudder. "Were they supposed to be out hunting in the middle of the day?"

"No, that's why this death is suspicious. The hunters are supposed to be out at dawn and dusk, but it's not like they all arrive and depart together," Sean explains. "The Palmyrton police are working in conjunction with the park police, who administer the hunting program. The hunters are all screened in advance before they can get permission to hunt in the park. It's competitive to get into the program—no wingnuts allowed. And they have to commit to staying in certain areas. Areas near the border of the park are too close to people's homes, so they're specifically excluded from hunting there. Yet the victim was killed on the trail that skirts near the Dupree home."

"So one of the hunters veered off course?" I give Aiden and Thea some apples after they start tossing their chicken to the dog.

Sean shakes his head. "They all claim to be exactly where they were supposed to be. And to have finished well before noon. They wear GPS devices that prove their locations."

"Can that be faked? Like leave your GPS somewhere while you go off where you want?"

"Possibly." Sean's face looks grim.

"You don't think it was an accident?" My eyes widen. "Say, could the victim have been one of the hunting protesters? Or could one of the protesters have killed him in order to disrupt the hunt?"

"We're looking into every angle. The victim wasn't married, didn't have kids, so it's taken us a while to track down friends and colleagues." Sean pops a sheet pan full of vegetables for our dinner into the oven. "But the people we've talked to so far were surprised to hear he was hiking in the park. Said he wasn't the outdoorsy type, so unlikely to have been a protester. But that hasn't been ruled out."

It had crossed my mind that the victim could be Bob Geary, the guy who knew Jeff Singleterry and visited the cottage during set-up, but he was definitely outdoorsy, a regular on the hiking trails. He must be safe. I release the kids from their chairs and set to work cleaning the mess they've left in their wake.

Sean holds up his hand. "Before you ask, the Public Affairs office is going to release the victim's name and photo tomorrow now that his next-of-kin has finally been located. They'll ask for the public's help—if anyone saw him in the park or knew why he was there."

I nudge Sean with my hip. "If Public Affairs is telling the world tomorrow, surely you can give me a little heads-up tonight."

Sean chuckles and pulls me into a hug. "Why does it matter to you?"

"Because someone was killed really close to where I was holding a sale on Saturday. He could've been one of my customers. I might recognize him."

Sean rolls his eyes, reluctant to admit I have a point. He takes his phone from his pocket and calls up an email, showing me the screen. "His name is Dermott O'Shea. He worked as an administrator for a small charity that helps struggling single mothers."

The middle-aged face staring back at me is pale and round with startled light blue eyes. His red hair is fading and thinning. He looks soft and kind and harmless.

And totally unfamiliar.

I shake my head. "I don't recognize him. But he looks sweet. I wonder why anyone would want to kill him?" As I set the table for our dinner, I continue to ruminate. "Maybe he was lured into the woods. Or he planned to meet someone there." I'm thinking aloud now, not really asking questions. "And then whoever wanted him there shot him with a bow and arrow to make it look like a hunting accident."

Sean chuckles and pats me on the knee. "Don't get ahead of yourself, Sherlock. We have a lot more investigating to do."

Chapter 17

Mornings have not been the same in our house since Thea figured out how to climb out of her crib. At first, we thought it was a one-time fluke, but then Sean caught her purposefully pulling herself over the bars and rappelling down the side like the guy climbing El Capitan in *Free Solo*. Aiden, unwilling to risk head trauma, watched and howled in outrage at his own captivity. Consequently, we had no choice but to put them both in toddler beds, which means the days of catching fifteen minutes of extra sleep while they played quietly and safely in their cribs are over.

When the twins wake up, their first order of business is to come and wake us up.

At 5:55 on Wednesday, I feel pudgy fingers poking my eye. "Mama, up. Let's play."

I emerge from sleep nose-to-nose with Aiden. Sean is still snoring lightly, so I intercept Thea on her path to the other side of the bed and herd both kids downstairs. No need for everyone to be up at this ungodly hour.

Diapers changed, Cheerios poured, coffee made, I pick up my phone which has been charging on the kitchen counter since I went to bed at ten last night. I've been sleeping better now that I keep the thing out of my bedroom at night.

Twenty-three text messages and five missed calls.

My heart turns over. Has something happened to my father? Has Natalie been trying to reach me? This is what happens when you swear off your phone to pay more attention to real life!

But no. The text messages are from a wide array of my friends and business associates. Many of them contain links.

Is this your estate sale?

OMG!

Have you seen this?

Holy crap, Audrey!

With a mounting sense of dread, I click one of the links. It leads to a video clip of a news story. A headline floats over the newscaster's head: **Five dollar trinket purchased at NJ estate sale worth big bucks.**

I turn on the audio. A chirpy woman newscaster in a lime green dress bares her white teeth at the camera and launches into her story. "Last week, a lucky customer at an estate sale in Palmyrton, New Jersey purchased a small, wooden house-shaped object for just five dollars. Today, it sold at Christie's auction house in Manhattan for a whopping $670,000. That's quite a mark-up! Here to tell us more is Alexander Wainthrop."

The camera switches to a distinguished-looking man in a silver-gray suit. Text beneath him says he's the medieval art specialist at Christie's.

My heart skips a beat.

He begins telling how someone sent in a photo of the object wondering if it might be valuable. While his voice drones in the background, the camera zooms in on a brown, wooden object, only slightly bigger than my coffee mug.

I relax a bit. It doesn't look familiar to me.

The expert continues, "I immediately recognized it as a reliquary—an artefact purported to contain a fragment of the bone of a saint, or a fragment of the cross on which Christ was crucified. Once we examined the object here in our workshop and carefully cleaned it, we determined that it dates from the 13th century. The craftsmanship and materials used indicate it came from southern Italy."

"And who is the lucky person who bought this at an estate sale?" the TV reporter asks.

I bring the phone closer to my face, trying to dig the information out.

"The seller does not wish to be identified."

"How do you know it's not fake?" the reporter presses.

"The seller purchased it from the estate of a noted medieval scholar, so we are confident it's authentic."

I fall back in my chair, the phone clattering onto the table. Aiden tosses a handful of Cheerios on the floor. Thea squeals as the dog comes to hoover them up.

$670,000! How could I have let this happen? I don't even recall seeing that little object, let alone pricing it at five bucks. It must've been Ty who priced it when he took over working on the cottage. But it's not his fault. I doubt I would have recognized the thing was old and valuable.

It looked like...nothing.

Seven hundred years old! Good lord! A medieval reliquary—how could any estate sale organizer be expected to recognize that?

"Ma!" Thea pounds her highchair tray, demanding to be released. Aiden squirms against his seatbelt.

Once I let the kids out to play, I can't afford to be distracted by work problems. So while they're still safely confined, I take a quick look at my list of missed calls.

Ty

Donna

Celeste Dupree

Katherine Dupree

Ty again.

I shut my eyes and knead my temples.

"Mama, OUT!"

Pushing my phone aside, I get up to tend to the twins. It's 6:30 in the morning—too early to call anyone—so I set the kids loose in the family room and sit on the rug to play with them.

As much as I try to focus on stacking blocks and zooming trucks, my mind keeps rolling back to the sale of Jefferson Singleterry's possessions. Why were his kids so reluctant to take their father's stuff? Why was Katherine so adamant that we find a way to give money to Matthew and Daphne? Did Jeff Singleterry know he possessed a rare artefact worth hundreds of thousands of dollars? And how the heck did he come to own it?

I rest my head on my knees. How am I going to explain this lapse to the Duprees?

"Mama sad?" Aiden lays his little hand on my cheek.

My heart swells with love for him. My children are safe. My husband is healthy. This will all work out.

I hope.

When Sean comes downstairs, the twins squeal and shout as if he's a rock star taking the stage. While he plays with them, I fix him a bowl of cereal and a cup of coffee and take another look at the photo of the reliquary. It looks like a little wooden house. A dusty old knick-knack.

Except that Jefferson Singleterry didn't have any knick-knacks in his house. That should have been our first clue.

If I had found it, would I have suspected it was something rare?

No, I can't let myself fall into the trap of "what if?" and "if only." I routinely delegate tasks to Ty and Donna. I can't be everywhere and do everything. There's no other way for me to run my business.

And yet...

Sean shovels down his breakfast with one eye on the clock as the twins clamber at his feet. "What's on your agenda today?" he asks.

I weigh my options. On one hand, I hate unloading this on Sean now when he's about to leave for a stressful day. But if random friends are texting me about the sale of the reliquary, Sean is bound to hear about it at work. I decide to tell him the bare minimum now and fill in the rest tonight when I know more.

"Uhm—I just found out we sold something at the Dupree sale for a lot less than it was worth, so I'll be dealing with those loose ends." Loose ends! I crack myself up with my gift for understatement.

Busy tickling Thea, Sean appears to have barely registered what I said. "Any new projects coming up?" he asks.

"Possibly. I need to visit a widow in Chatham who's moving to South Carolina."

"Can she take us with her? Between my boss and my brother, I'm ready for a change of scenery."

I pat him on the back. "You'd never leave Palmyrton."

Sean says nothing. Just kisses me and the kids good-bye and heads out the door as Roseline shows up.

She immediately starts cleaning up our breakfast mess. Normally, I'd help, but today I need to prepare myself to face the day.

I text Ty and Donna and tell them to meet me at the office by eight. This is too important to discuss on the phone.

As soon as I step out of the shower, my phone starts ringing.

Celeste Dupree. I take a deep breath and answer.

"Hello, Audrey." Her voice is icy. She doesn't bother with any "how are yous?" or "have you seen the news?" She goes straight to the heart of the matter. "I've had several calls from Matthew and Daphne Singleterry. As you can imagine, they're quite upset. I'm in San Jose now, but I plan to fly back to New Jersey tonight." She heaves a sigh of irritation. "I need to schedule a meeting with you tomorrow. In the meantime, I ask you not to talk to my mother or the Singleterrys."

"Of course. I'm happy to meet any time." I take a steadying breath. "Celeste, I'm really sorry. Nothing like this has ever happened to our company before. We had no idea—"

"I'd also like to discuss the cash you...fo-o-o-und...in Jeff's garden statue."

The way she drawls out "found" tells me the jig is up. Matthew and Daphne must have told her about the money. I can't even form a response.

"I'll see you at your office at eleven tomorrow morning," Celeste snaps. "Remember, don't talk to Mother, Matthew, or Daphne."

Click.

I stare at my flushed face in the bathroom mirror. It could've been worse. I'd rather deal with cold anger than hot hysteria. A meeting tomorrow gives me time today to gather as much information as possible in preparation.

I do wonder at Celeste's prohibition about talking to anyone else before I talk to her. On one hand, she's naturally a logical, take-charge person. Talking to the Singleterry siblings will be an emotional whirlwind I'd just as soon avoid. But I do wonder about Celeste's motivations. Is she committed to doing the best for everyone involved?

Or just covering her own ass?

Does Celeste already know the money we "discovered" at Jeff's house was her mother's idea? Last week, that kind-hearted deception seemed harmless; today, it's fraught with problems. Am I supposed to keep Mrs. Dupree's secret when I speak to Celeste tomorrow? I was willing to help the old gal out, but I'm not willing to take the fall for her.

I'll discuss the Katherine Dupree situation with Ty and Donna and get their advice.

It will be easy enough to duck Mrs. Dupree. Let's hope Matthew and Daphne don't track me down.

When I arrive at the office, Ty pounces on me as soon as I walk through the door.

"Audge, what the hell? My phone blew up last night!" Ty paces across from his desk to mine. "The whole world knows about this! I got texts from people I haven't talked to in years."

"Have you heard from Carter Lemoine?"

"Yeah, he says he doesn't personally know Wainthorp, the guy interviewed on TV. But he says the guy is a heads-up dude, knows his stuff."

"Too bad. Professional error would have been our best outcome, but I'm sure Christie's wouldn't have released this to the mainstream news if they weren't absolutely certain the reliquary is authentic."

Ty bangs his clenched fist on the window trim as he passes. "This is all my fault. I'm the one who priced it at five bucks."

I step in front of Ty and grab his face between my hands. "Listen to me. This is not your fault. No one could've known what that thing was, and we certainly couldn't have known what it was worth."

"Yeah," Donna chimes in. "I've never even heard of a reliquary, and I'm Catholic!"

But Ty isn't letting himself off the hook that easy. "I lost us a ton of money. And I lost Matthew and Daphne even more. They're not going to let this go with 'finders, keepers.'"

This is precisely what's worrying me and Celeste. I tell my staff about my meeting with Mrs. Dupree's daughter tomorrow. "I want us to brainstorm now and gather as much information as possible so I'm prepared."

Donna's forehead creases with worry. "Are you personally in trouble for this, Audrey?"

"Legal trouble? I doubt it, but I'll call our lawyer later today." I don't want to share the rest of my thoughts. Despite the fact that an estate sale organizer can't be expected to know about a specialized box for saints' bones, this incident doesn't look good for Another Man's Treasure. We'll forever be remembered as the firm that let a super-valuable item slip away for five bucks.

Donna lets out a gust of air that blows her long bangs off her brow. "How can they be mad at us? Both Jeff's kids and Mrs. Dupree said there was nothing of value in the cottage. No one said, "Keep an eye peeled for priceless medieval artefacts."

"Do you remember where the reliquary was in the cottage? Was it hidden away?" I ask Ty.

Ty shakes his head. "I found it in the kitchen, on a shelf with some other odds and ends. A cheese grater. Some empty Mason jars. I remember wondering if it was some kinda spice container or something because the roof lifted off. The wood seemed pretty solid and the carving was nice, so I figured maybe someone would take it for five bucks and clean it up."

"What was inside?" Donna whispers.

"Just dust. No bones, believe me."

I lean forward with more urgency. "Who bought it?"

Ty rubs his eyes. "I've been bustin' my brain tryin' to remember. But I keep coming up blank."

I pat Ty's shoulder. "Relax. It might pop into your mind when you least expect it."

Donna taps a pencil on her desk. "Here's what bothers me. Estate sale patrons are always alert for a bargain, but the average person on the prowl for Depression glass and Fiesta Ware isn't likely to recognize medieval art. Someone must've come to that sale because they knew who Jeff was and thought he might have something worthwhile."

"Not just thought it," I say. "The buyer must've *known*. Jeff must've shown it to someone or boasted about having it." I rake my hands through my hair.

Ty sighs. "Honestly, most people who came down to the cottage were just exploring the Dupree's yard, not looking to buy anything specific. They wandered down the stone path from the big house, and I could hear them all callin' out." Ty raises the pitch of his voice to imitate excited ladies. "'Oh, look at this cute little house!' 'How cool that it's tucked in the woods. Let's go in.'"

"But once they were inside, they did buy things," Donna reminds him.

Ty extends his hands. "You know our customers. They almost always find somethin' they gonna buy, no matter where they are."

It's Ty's theory that half of our work is redistributing clutter from one hoarder to another.

I lean forward. "So no one seemed like they came there intentionally? Like they were on a mission?"

"Just that early bird dude who was buggin' you during set-up," Ty says. "He came in from the woods, all dressed up in his hiking gear."

Bob! Of course! I'd forgotten about him. My voice rises in excitement. "He was very interested in Jeff and knew all about his medieval studies. And he kept trying to peek inside the cottage. It must've been him who bought the reliquary."

Ty shakes his head. "Nope. I remember him cuz he never shut up the whole time he was there. Talkin' to the other customers, talkin' to me." Ty clacks his fingers like jaws. "He bought some books, that's all."

Another thought pops into my head. The man who was shot with an arrow in the woods near the Dupree home—could he have bought the reliquary and then.... what? Someone stole it from him and sold it. A little far-fetched, but it would explain why the seller wants to remain incognito.

Sean told me the police were going to go public with the victim's identity today. I navigate to the *Palmyrton Now!* news website, and there's a picture of Dermott O'Shea and a plea for help from the public. I show the photo to Ty and Donna. "This was the man who was shot in the woods with an arrow. Does he look familiar to you? Was he at the sale?"

Donna puts a finger to her chin and slowly shakes her head. "I don't think so. If he was there, he definitely didn't buy anything from me."

Ty takes my phone in his long, strong hands and studies the face that fills the screen. Eventually, he also shakes his head. "He didn't come to the cottage during the sale. You know I have a good memory for faces, and those bulgy eyes of his would stick with me."

"Hey!" Donna exclaims. "Todd Dupree was at the sale at the big house and we never noticed him leave. Remember, Audrey—we said he must've gone out the back and down to the cottage. Maybe he bought the reliquary."

I turn to Ty. "Do you remember seeing a man who looks just like the young Gaston Dupree?"

Ty snaps his fingers. "I knew that dude looked familiar! I kept trying to remember where I'd met him before, but it was that photo of Mr. Dupree that he resembled. So that's Katherine's son, eh?"

"Yes." My voice rises in excitement. "So he did go down to the cottage. Could he have bought the reliquary?"

Ty shakes his head. "Nah—he showed up late, right before I was ready to close up. He came in talking, so I expected another person to follow him in. But he was alone—just talking to himself, I guess. He looked around, muttered something under his breath, and left. Kind of a strange dude."

Another possible lead ruled out. "What about a receipt?" I ask Ty. "Did anyone ask you for one? The buyer would need it to establish provenance."

Most customers who buy inexpensive items for personal use don't want a receipt, so we only hand them out upon request. But dealers who are buying items they intend to resell almost always want a receipt. Our blank receipts have Another Man's Treasure Estate Sales printed at the top, with room for the date, a list of items and their prices, a total with tax, and a spot for the initials of the seller.

"Gimme the receipt book, Donna," Ty demands.

He flips back through the carbon copies and finds two receipts with the correct date and "Singleterry" scrawled at the top to distinguish it from all the receipts handed out from the Dupree sale. Ty taps the pad. "This one I remember. Five hardcover books for ten dollars. The lady was buying them for her friend and wanted a receipt so she could be reimbursed."

Donna peers over his shoulder. "You're not going to find one that says 'ancient reliquary' since you didn't even know what it was."

Ty's hand pauses on a receipt. "This is it," he whispers. "Garden tool, coffee mug, box. Seven-fifty, total."

Donna and I stare at him, waiting for more.

Ty stretches back in the chair, his long body at a forty-five degree angle to the floor, his eyes clenched tight in concentration. "It was after the book lady asked for a receipt. Close to lunch time. I was hungry. I was bored not being up at the big house, so I was texting with a friend." He groans, angry at himself. "I can't picture the person who asked for the receipt. I just wasn't paying attention."

Ty opens his big, brown eyes and gazes at me. "I'm so sorry, Audge."

Chapter 18

We all sit in silence. After a few minutes, Donna speaks up. "Does it really matter who bought it? I mean, what the buyer did was legal. They bought an item for the price we were charging. Then they sold it for more. It happens all the time, just not on such a big scale."

"It's not illegal," I agree. "But there's something suspicious about this deal. If we could prove that the person who bought the reliquary knew it was there and intentionally withheld that information from the rightful heirs, then Jeff's children might have good shot at a lawsuit to claw some of the money back."

"But nothing for us," Ty says grimly. "Twenty percent of $670,000 is..." He fishes for his calculator.

"$134,000," I say. "Don't even think about it. We went into Mr. Singleterry's sale expecting nothing, and that's what we got. We should be happy that we did so well on the Dupree sale."

"Why you takin' this so good?" Ty asks.

"The money seems unreal, theoretical," I answer. "I'm more worried about the hit to our reputation. It will take Another Man's Treasure a while to live down the scandal of selling a valuable artefact for five bucks. What's worse is that because we found cash in Mr. Singleterry's house that wasn't really there, now it looks like we were running some kind of scam."

Ty's brows draw down. "I didn't think of that. It looks like, 'good news—we found twenty grand hidden in your dad's house. Bad news—we sold his half-million dollar reliquary for five bucks.'"

"Exactly. That's the most important reason I want to discover who bought it—so I can prove we aren't in cahoots with him. And then there's the matter of explaining this to Celeste Dupree."

"You're gonna tell her the truth about the cash we discovered for Jeff's kids?" Ty's eyes open wide. "You're gonna throw Katherine under the bus?"

Ty lives by a strict no-snitching code, so I knew this wouldn't go down well with him. I massage my temples. "I don't see a way around it. I never should have agreed to Katherine's scheme in the first place, but it seemed so harmless. Now I'm caught in the middle of a big lie. When will I ever learn?"

Ty scowls but remains silent. He's not in a position to argue with me since he thinks he screwed-up, but I can see that he disapproves of my decision to break Katherine's trust especially since none of us really likes Celeste. "How would you handle it?" I ask. "I don't want to tell more lies to cover up the initial lie."

"Well, at least call Katherine and give her a heads-up," Ty says.

I sigh. "Celeste specifically warned me not to talk to her mother before our meeting."

Ty slaps the desk. "See! She's cookin' up trouble behind her mother's back." He spins in his desk chair. "Katherine should have the right to give some money to her friend's kids if she wants to. She's not senile. In fact, she's really sharp. I like the old gal."

I feel a rock settle in the pit of my stomach. I like Katherine, too.

And now I'm going to betray her.

Chapter 19

Sean arrives home from work and greets me with a quizzical expression on his face. "A reliquary worth nearly three quarters of a million bucks? That's what you sold for five bucks?"

I plop down at the kitchen table and cradle my head in my hands. "So, you heard."

"I heard from a dozen other cops. Why didn't you tell me this morning?"

"I'm sorry. I didn't want to worry you when there was nothing you could do to help. I know more now." While Sean and I work on making dinner, I tell him everything I know about the reliquary sale, ending with, "And Ty can't remember who he sold it to. But I'm sure the person who bought it came to the sale looking for it. No random estate sale customer could recognize something so obscure and get it auctioned off at Christie's so quickly. I'm going to find out who it was so I can salvage my reputation."

Sean frowns as he dumps a bag of salad greens into a bowl. I'm not sure if he's displeased by the number of wilted leaves or by my latest investigative plan. "What does Mrs. Dupree have to say? How can it be your fault if she had no idea her tenant possessed something so valuable?"

"I doubt Katherine blames me." Then I take a deep breath and tell Sean about Katherine's request that we "discover" money that she could give to Jeff's kids.

He stops shaking the salad dressing and slowly sets the bottle on the counter, his eyes wide with incredulity. "Seriously? You agreed to a stunt like that?"

"It seemed harmless enough." I turn to place the silverware on the table so I can avoid Sean's gaze. "She wouldn't have given us the job if we didn't agree to help her out in channeling some cash to the Singleterrys."

Sean tosses the salad with brutal vigor. Before he can reproach me, I pull the salad bowl away and put it on the table. "I have a meeting with Celeste Dupree tomorrow morning. I'll explain everything and hopefully she'll have some ideas on how to proceed." I pat Sean's chair. "Now, sit down and tell me the latest on your brother."

There's nothing like Coughlin family drama to divert the heat away from me. Sean launches into a long tale of woe about how Terry is in really deep doo-doo because the guy whose wallet he lifted is a lawyer with a big firm in Newark. "He's pressuring the district attorney to charge Terry with the highest felony charges." Sean arches his back until it cracks. "Meanwhile I'm trying to use all my contacts to get the DA to reduce the charges. But what my family doesn't understand is that if I push too hard, it could backfire. The DA doesn't want to look like he caves in to the demands of the police when the accused has connections on the force." He gazes up at the ceiling. "I honestly don't know where his case will land."

"You think Terry could actually be sent to jail?" That's a possibility too horrifying to contemplate.

Sean pushes his food listlessly around his plate. "I could live with Terry doing time if I didn't think it would kill my parents."

I make a mental note not to accept any calls from my mother-in-law or sisters-in-law. I won't be able to offer the sympathy they seek, and they'll be offended by any response that isn't one-hundred-and-ten percent behind Terry.

Once again, I change the subject. "Say, did you find the arrow I threw in the Dupree's trash?"

Sean brightens. "We did. The shaft has a lot of smeared partial prints."

"The little kid who found it had his grubby mitts all over it, and then his mother had to wrestle it away from him. And I touched it when I threw it out." I flex my fingers. "Do you need to take my prints for elimination purposes?"

Sean smiles at my eagerness. "We'll see. Right now, the lab is testing the blood on the tip to see if it's animal or human." Sean arches his eyebrows. "But here's an interesting tidbit. That type of arrow isn't one of the approved types for the hunting program."

My eyes widen. "And does it match the arrow found in Dermott O'Shea's body?"

"It does."

Chapter 20

The next morning, I send Donna and Ty to provide an assessment on a routine sale for a new client so that I'm alone in the office when Celeste arrives for our meeting.

At the stroke of ten, I hear a sharp rap on the door and before I can answer, Celeste Dupree storms in. She starts talking immediately in a low, seething voice. "I was given to understand that you are a professional, Ms. Nealon. Instead, I find that you allowed a valuable artifact to be sold for a pittance while at the same time taking advantage of the good nature of an elderly disabled woman. I want an explanation before I call my lawyer, and possibly, the police."

I know her threats are empty, but I'm still upset and unnerved. I decide to tackle the found cash issue first. "I did not take advantage of anyone. Your mother asked me to do her a favor, Celeste. It seemed harmless enough."

"Harmless to deceive me?" Celeste's voice rises and she thumbs her own chest. "I have her power of attorney for a reason. My father knew she isn't capable of managing her financial affairs."

"I didn't know about your financial affairs. She seems perfectly lucid to me. And she said she wanted to give Matthew and Daphne the money this way so it didn't seem like a handout, not to deceive you. She knew you'd find out soon enough."

Celeste wags her finger at me. "You've known my mother for a week, Ms. Nealon. I've known her for 54 years. This isn't the first time she's done something like this." Celeste drops into my visitor's chair. "She collects strays—stray animals, stray people. My father's friendship with Jeff Singleterry probably would've dissolved decades ago, but my mother kept it going because she felt sorry for Jeff. And now she feels sorry for his dysfunctional children. If she gave twenty thousand dollars to every lost soul she encountered, she really would be destitute."

I think about the homely one-eyed cat and the dying houseplant she wouldn't discard. I guess Mrs. Dupree really is a lover of lost causes.

But I also remember what I learned from Todd Dupree at the sale. His parents' marriage wasn't as happy as it was presented to the outside world. Maybe all the "help" Gaston offered was really a way to control Katherine, and Celeste is picking up where her father left off. Todd suggested that Celeste strong-armed Katherine into moving. At the time Todd said it, I thought he was lashing out. Now I'm not so sure.

Not that I can say any of that right now. Instead, I float a statement of fact to test Celeste's reaction. "I met your brother Todd at the sale. He seemed surprised that it was happening. Did you not both agree that the house should be sold?"

Celeste jerks as if she's been slapped. "Todd came to the sale?"

"Yes. He introduced himself to me. Said he only learned of the sale a couple days before it happened."

Celeste snorts. "Typical Todd. His head is in another world. He doesn't listen to a thing I say, then he claims he never knew." She shakes her head. "I can't believe he was in New Jersey and didn't visit our mother." Then Celeste throws back her shoulders and narrows her eyes. "None of this has anything to do with the lie you told about finding money at Jeff's house. Now Daphne and Matthew have gone from being thrilled by their cash windfall to being sure that they were swindled out of their rightful inheritance." Celeste swings her crossed leg. "Do you see how bad this looks for me and my mother?"

"Yes, I, I—"

Celeste's large, capable hands grip the armrests of her chair. "You've lied about the cash, which makes me suspect you lied about the reliquary as well."

Outrage wells up inside me, but I swallow it down. I have no right to be offended; I need to earn back Celeste's trust. "Look, I would never have agreed to hold a sale at the cottage if it weren't for the fact that the sale at the main house was bound to be very profitable. I did the cottage as a favor to you and your mom to clear it out. Neither of you thought Mr. Singleterry had anything of value. Your mom mentioned he was an academic, but I didn't even know his area of expertise. How could I possibly have recognized that nondescript little box as a valuable medieval artefact? Most people don't even know what reliquaries are."

Celeste doesn't answer. Her chest rises and falls as if she's just run for the bus. "You're not *most people*, Ms. Nealon," she hisses. "You promote yourself as having a knowledge of art and antiques."

I can't contain my irritation. "I'm very well versed in the kinds of art and antiques I'm likely to encounter in a private home. Who do you know who keeps containers of dead saints' bones around the house?"

We glare at each other. Suddenly, Celeste bursts into bitter laughter, cradling her head in her hands. "Everyone warned me moving my mother into assisted living would be difficult, but who could have anticipated this mess? My life is spinning out of control."

I see an opening here. Celeste is a take-charge-person, used to managing, not being manipulated. I can use that. "I'm really sorry for saying we discovered cash in the house, Celeste. But even though I feel terrible about the reliquary, I stand firm in my position that Another Man's Treasure bears no legal responsibility for the fact that we sold it far below market value." Celeste opens her mouth to argue, but I keep talking. "However, I want to try to make things right for the Singleterry heirs. Whoever bought that reliquary knew exactly what it was because they took it directly to Christie's. That makes me suspect it was another medieval scholar, someone who knew Jeff professionally. Christie's won't reveal who brought them the reliquary, but if you and I could figure out who it was, a good lawyer might be able to claw back some of the money for Matthew and Daphne."

Celeste looks intrigued. "Hmmm. If it was someone with an academic reputation to protect, they might be willing to settle. The threat of a lawsuit is often enough to produce results."

"Matthew Singleterry told me your mom used to help Jeff email his academic articles to journals. Maybe she'd know some of his contacts in the medieval history field."

"Good thought. I'll ask her and let you know what I come up with."

I can practically see the wheels turning in her head, so I keep my mouth shut and wait to see what else she'll come up with.

"Nabbing that piece from the estate of a poor man, knowing full well that it was valuable could create a social media firestorm." Celeste grins. "And I know some people in Silicon Valley who are pretty good at igniting a few flames."

———◆———

TY AND DONNA RETURN from their client visit and slip wordlessly into their desk chairs.

"What's wrong with you two? Run over another racoon?"

Donna shoots Ty a look that clearly says, "Shall I tell her or will you?"

"We didn't get the job," Ty says.

"No need to take it so hard. We win some, we lose some." I return to analyzing my spreadsheet. But the thick silence in the office makes me look up within a minute, and I see the two of them mouthing words and trading hand signals. "Is there more you need to tell me?"

"Oh, Audrey, it was awful!" Donna begins. "The lady kept asking us about the reliquary and how could we guarantee that we wouldn't sell something of hers for way less than it's worth."

"She didn't even have anything good," Ty grumbles. "But I explained how we operate—"

"He did it really well," Donna says. "I was getting rattled, but not Ty."

Ty leans forward with his elbows on his knees and speaks while gazing at the floor. "She wouldn't let up about all the news she read about the Dupree sale. It was like she already had her mind made up against us before we even got there." Ty lifts his head. "I fought to make it right with her, but she just wouldn't listen."

"It's okay," I say in the tone I use to soothe my kids. "Don't worry about it." But I'm worried. Thanksgiving through Christmas is always our slow season. I was hoping to get in two more good sales in November, but it looks like that might not happen this year.

Ty stands and puts on his best basketball coach face. "Imma find a way to make this right."

I appreciate his fierce determination, but I suspect time is the only way to erase the negative publicity of our reliquary disaster.

Chapter 21

Two days have gone by with no word from Celeste about whether her mother has contacts for any of Jeff's academic colleagues. Two long days in which the reliquary story has stayed in the news although not on the front page. Alone in the office, I fret and fidget, unable to focus on my routine tasks.

I thought Celeste shared my enthusiasm for finding the person who bought the reliquary, but now I'm not so sure. I don't like relying on someone else to take action. I'd rather contact Mrs. Dupree myself. But I promised Celeste I wouldn't talk to her mother, so I call the daughter instead. Before I can say a word, Celeste starts talking.

"Audrey! Perfect timing." Her voice has an echo-y quality, so I assume she's driving while talking. "Listen, I talked to my mother about the people she sent emails to on Jeff's behalf. She says she always deleted them after she received acknowledgement that they got the document. So that's a dead end. But she did tell me the two colleges Jeff taught at most recently, so you could follow up on that. I'll text you the names as soon as I get back to my office."

I'm disappointed the emails didn't pan out—that seemed like such a promising lead. "Okay. So, you're back in California now?"

"Yes. I couldn't afford to be away from work for long."

That means I'm going to have to do the work of tracking down whoever bought the reliquary. Which is fine. I just need Celeste to step out of my way. "Where did you leave matters with your mother...er...regarding Matthew and Daphne and the money?"

"Leave the Singleterrys to me." The familiar haughtiness returns to Celeste's voice. "You just follow up on those colleges." A loud screech of horns and sirens comes through the line. "Gotta go. Text you later."

I look at the silent phone in my hand. Dismissed.

Across the office, a stack of Jeff Singleterry's unsold books taunts me. I go over and start leafing through one: *Medieval Mystics and Herbalists—Sickness of the Body and the Spirit*. Tiny type, dense prose—I just can't. I pick up another. This one has illustrations of medicinal plants. I'm studying the identification of various plants when my phone chirps the arrival of a text. Seven words from Celeste: Sussex Community College, College of Saint Joan.

Celeste has given me an assignment, so I might as well jump on it. I call Sussex Community College and mange to connect with the Chair of the history department without much delay. When I explain I'm calling in reference to Jefferson Singleterry, his voice grows cool. "I heard that he passed away. Very sad."

He doesn't sound at all heartbroken. "Are there any colleagues in the history department who shared his passion for medieval religious history? Or perhaps a special student he inspired?"

The chairman guffaws as if I were the guest star on a late-night comedy show. "We're a community college, Ms. Nealon. We call it a win if most of our students graduate knowing in which century the American Civil War took place. I know that Jeff Singleterry wrote his PhD thesis on some topic in medieval history, but that's not what he taught here. He was assigned a basic survey course, Introduction to European History."

Okay, so not a student. But there might still be another professor who shared Jeff's interests. "I understand your college doesn't offer a lot of highly specialized history classes, but I'm hoping to locate a colleague that knew Jeff well...knew about his passions."

"Humpf. I doubt anyone here fills that role. Jeff was argumentative and condescending, so not popular with the faculty, the staff, or the students. If he hadn't died over the summer, I wouldn't have hired him back for this academic year."

Another dead end. With dwindling hope, I call the other college where Jeff taught last academic year, The College of Saint Joan. According to their website, the school was founded to train young women to be parochial schoolteachers. It's co-ed now, but still has a big program for education majors. It seems more plausible that I could find a medieval religious scholar here. After being transferred several times, I wind up talking to a Professor Healy, an art history professor. I don't have to say more than "estate sale" to trigger an outpouring of information.

"Ah, you're the one who sold Jeff's reliquary!" Professor Healy chortles. "Frankly, I thought the thing was a figment of his imagination, but it looks like I was wrong."

My heart skips a beat. "Jeff talked to you openly about the reliquary?"

"Oh, yes. Ad nauseum. As an art historian, I'm more interested in the artistic workmanship of reliquaries. Many are made from gold and silver and precious gems. This wooden one wasn't particularly spectacular. But I let Jeff tell me all about it."

Now I'm getting somewhere! "Did you ever see it?"

"He showed me a photo once. Just a blurry old snapshot. Looked like it was taken with an Instamatic. You're probably too young to remember those."

"Did you ever see it at his home?"

Healy makes a raspberry sound. "I wouldn't drive fifty minutes to Palmyrton to visit Jeff Singleterry. I found him amusing to talk to here on campus, but we weren't beer-drinking buddies. And as I said, the reliquary wasn't an extraordinary piece of art."

"So you didn't come to the estate sale looking for it?" I ask point blank.

"Me?" he squeaks. "You think I'm the one who bought it for five bucks and sold it for three-quarters of a million? I wish! I wouldn't be grinding away correcting exams here in my office if I came into that windfall."

Maybe—although a million bucks doesn't go as far as it used to.

Healy keeps talking without further encouragement from me. "No, I have no time for estate sales. I spend every Saturday tutoring high school students trying to pass their AP History exam."

I might have known this colleague of Jeff's wouldn't be chatting with me if he were the buyer. I move on. "Do you know how Jeff happened to acquire the reliquary?"

"Nope. When I asked, he'd clam up. That's why I thought he was lying about owning it. I thought he'd simply taken a picture of it in a museum, and then boasted it was his. Guess I was wrong."

"Did he ever mention wanting to sell it? Say that he had someone interested in buying it?" I listen carefully to Healy's response. Despite his dismissive tone, I still suspect he might be the buyer.

"Oh, heavens, no! Jeff would never have sold it." Healy emphasizes the word 'sold' as if this were a bizarre concept. "He didn't care about money. For him, the reliquary had enormous *spiritual* value."

"I see." I say this even though I really don't see at all. Could a highly educated man like Jeff Singleterry really believe that a fragment of a saint's bone had some magical power? Besides, the reliquary was empty. You can't expect a box that's been kicking around for seven hundred years to still contain its original contents, whatever they may have been. "I'm sorry to sound sacrilegious, but could you explain to me the power the object held for him? You see, it was empty when we put it in the sale, so..."

"Empty? Surely not!" Healy sounds incredulous. Then he gasps. "You didn't *wipe it clean* before you sold it, did you?"

"Uh...no. My assistant said the inside was just a bit dusty."

"Ah, but that was no ordinary dust, young lady. Perhaps it was soil from the Mount of Olives, or a twig from the burning bush."

He chuckles and I can't be sure if he's serious or pulling my leg. I wish I was talking to him in person instead of on the phone. "Prof. Healy, my unintentional sale of this valuable reliquary may seem amusing to you, but it's serious business for me. I'm trying to understand what it meant to Jeff, and who else knew he had it. I believe the person who bought it knew exactly what it was when they bought it for five bucks. They've cheated Jeff's heirs out of their rightful inheritance."

"Huh...interesting that you should say that." The bantering tone disappears from his voice, and he starts to show some scholarly interest. "You see, in medieval society, reliquaries were often a form of currency, handed down through the generations or included as part of a dowry. And they'd sometimes be donated to a church as way to barter for prayers. I believe that was Jeff's plan."

This is interesting, but I'm not quite making the connection I should be. "What was Jeff's plan?"

"Sometimes when Jeff would really get rolling on the topic of that reliquary, I'd sort of tune him out, but I do recall that he wanted the reliquary to reside in a sacred place." Healy pauses, clears his throat, and resumes. "As I mentioned, I didn't entirely believe Jeff actually possessed the thing, so sometimes I'd sort of goad him and ask if he'd found the proper monastery to give it to yet."

I'm beginning to dislike Prof. Healy. He was probably the kind of kid who enjoyed pulling the wings off flies. "And what did he reply?"

"He'd tell me, 'not yet, but soon.' Now it seems that time ran out on Jeff. He died before he could give the reliquary to a religious institution." Healy gives another snide chuckle. "Guess that means he's missed out on all the prayers it could have bought!"

After I end the call with Healy, I sit staring at my phone. If Jeff never intended to sell the reliquary or leave it to his kids...if he intended to bequeath it to a church...does that change my responsibility? Instead of Matthew and Daphne being deprived of their inheritance, some nameless monastery came up short. And did Jeff really intend to pay the monks to pray for his eternal soul? Did that still happen in the 21st century?

Now I really want to talk to Mrs. Dupree. If Jeff told Prof. Healy—a rather indifferent colleague—about the reliquary, surely he would've also told his good friend, Katherine.

Maybe now that I have some solid evidence to offer Celeste, she'll agree to my visiting her mother. I send her a quick email outlining my conversation with Prof. Healy and end it with, "I'd like to review this with your mother."

Celeste's reply pings back into my inbox at warp speed. "Interesting information on Healy. I'll see if I can find out more about him. My mother is not seeing visitors. The adjustment to Shadow Glen has been difficult for her. Emotional stress always makes the symptoms of her multiple sclerosis worse. She mustn't be bothered this week."

I sigh as I reread the email. I can't blame Celeste for safeguarding her mother's health. I would do the same for my father.

But Katherine's enforced silence sure does make my work harder. As long as I have Celeste's attention, I reply again, asking where things stand with the Singleterrys.

I expect another quick reply, but the afternoon passes with nothing further from Celeste.

As the day ends, Ty sits with his feet up on his desk, trying to type while balancing his laptop on his knees. Donna vacuums under and around him, then moves to the other side of the office. "Ty, this pile of electronics has been here for-EV-uh. I thought you were taking it to recycling."

Ty waves her off. "I'll take it on Monday."

"You're such a procrastinator," Donna complains. "Just take—"

My head snaps up. "Wait. Is Jeff Singleterry's computer still here?"

"Yes, at the bottom of the heap."

I jump up and scurry to the tower of electronics. "Oh, wow! Why didn't you remind me of this?"

Donna scratches her head. "Remind you? Why?"

"Maybe Jeff Singleterry's computer contains some information on who else knew about the reliquary." I start shifting the old DVD players and an LP turntable. "Come on, Ty—help me get it out and set it up."

Half an hour later, the old clunker hums and coughs to life. A blue line appears on the monitor and finally spreads across the screen. A little light pulses behind a cursor in the bottom corner."

"Where are the icons?" Ty asks.

"I think It's running an ancient operating system," I say.

That means it's not password protected, but it's so old none of us knows how to launch the word-processing program or open any files. Donna pulls out her phone and takes a picture. "I'm going to send this to my Uncle Vinny. I bet he'll know what to do."

"Can't believe you actually have an Uncle Vinny," Ty mutters.

The gods are smiling on us because Uncle Vinny does, in fact, know how to operate this dinosaur. A few keystrokes later, a long list of documents fills the screen.

Ty peers over my shoulder at the cryptic document names, each one a meaningless series of numbers and letters. "I guess it'd be asking too much for him to name the document, 'article about priceless reliquary,'" he grumbles.

I click open the most recent document, a maddeningly slow process on this old machine. Single-spaced paragraphs fill the screen. I read the first two sentences, which contain four multisyllabic words that I'd need to look up. My heart sinks. It could take me weeks to comb through the dense academic prose in all these documents.

Ty and Donna drift away.

But what choice do I have? This computer contains the only possible insights into Jefferson Singleterry's life and work.

Then I get an idea. Maybe my dad could do it for me. Painstaking research is right up his alley. I dial his number.

"Dad, I have a research project for you." As soon as he answers, I make this announcement with a determinedly cheery voice.

"Oh?" My father knows me well enough to respond with caution.

I explain that I need him to comb through dense academic articles on religious history residing on an ancient computer. When I realize how utterly unappealing that sounds, I add, "Please help me, Dad. I need to find out who bought that reliquary to save the reputation of Another Man's Treasure. This could provide a clue, but if I try to do it myself after the kids are in bed, it'll take me months."

"Okay, bring it over. As it happens, I have something I need to discuss with you."

Chapter 22

I arrive at my father's place to find him bustling about making tea and setting out cookies, a domestic task I've rarely seen him perform. Even though his wife Natalie had a long career as a nurse practitioner, she dotes on my father in retirement. He steps spryly around the condo while his cane rests unused in a corner.

"Natalie's at aqua aerobics," he explains. "What's this research project you've got for me?" He rubs his hands in anticipation.

Pulling out the flash drive that contains the academic articles from Jeff's computer, I plug it into my father's laptop and start explaining what I need Dad to do. "Jeff Singleterry was a scholar of medieval religious history. He wrote all these articles for obscure academic journals. I don't have time to wade through them all, but I thought you might be able to pick out a theme in the articles or find some mention of reliquaries and their significance."

My father has a slightly distasteful expression on his face, so I head off his objection before he can speak. "Look, I know religious history isn't your favorite, but I think Jeff was also interested in medieval healers and herbalists. That could be significant because it seems he died from kidney failure that might have been brought on from an herbal remedy."

Dad frowns over his yellow legal pad. "Your instructions are rather vague, Audrey. What exactly am I looking for?"

"You'll know it when you see it" is not the kind of guidance I can give to my uber-logical father. But that's the nature of searching for clues. The significance of each factoid often isn't clear until it's slotted into a larger picture. I can't expect my father to find the needle in the haystack, but he might be able to take some hay out of the haystack to make the needle easier to spot. "If you can just highlight all the sections on reliquaries and herbalism, that would help me. Then I can read over just those sections to see if I find anything significant." I tap his hand as it hovers with a poised pen. "You have experience cutting through all the falderol in scholarly writing."

Dad straightens his shoulders to prepare for battle. "That I do. I'll get to work this afternoon. It'll probably take me about three days."

"Perfect!" I kiss his cheek. "That's ten times faster than I could do it. Now, what was it you wanted to discuss with me?"

Dad takes a sip from his mug of tea. "The tests the neurologist ran this week indicate that I've had a few mini strokes. There's nothing they can do about them, no long-lasting damage. But it's a bad sign for the future. I could have another massive stroke at any time." Dad speaks calmly, as if he's discussing a stranger's ailments.

"But it doesn't mean you absolutely will have another stroke," I object. "Look how steady you've become on your feet. All that Tai Chi is paying off."

"We have to be realistic, Audrey. The odds are, I will. And that's what I want to talk to you about." He locks his gaze with mine. "If...when...it happens, I don't want any extraordinary measures taken. I'm ten years older than I was when I had my first stroke. I won't be able to fight my way back from another one, and I don't want to live as an invalid in a nursing home." He shivers, and I know he's remembering the time he spent at the Manor View Senior Living Center, a terrible, despairing place.

"Natalie and I would never send you to a nursing home," I reassure him. So much has changed between us since that first stroke. And Dad has so much more to live for now than he did then.

"I don't want to be a burden on you and Natalie. That would be even worse than being in a home. I have a Do Not Resuscitate order in my will. Natalie has promised to honor my wishes. No CPR, no shocks, no tubes. Now I want you to do the same. Promise me."

I pull away. I don't want to talk about this, don't want to face it. I'm not ready to lose my father. "I still need you, Dad," I whisper.

"You have a wonderful husband, two beautiful children, loving in-laws. You'll be fine without me."

Why does he always have to be so logical? Why can't he acknowledge my pain? "They can't replace you!" My voice comes out louder and angrier than I intended.

Dad just smiles. "They won't replace me, but they'll be there to support you. I'll be no use to you lying in a bed, wired up to machines." He takes my hands in his. "I've had a good run, Audrey. Let me exit this life with dignity. Please."

We stand holding hands for a long while.

Finally, I whisper, "I promise."

Chapter 23

On the drive home, I crank up the volume on my radio to let Bruce Springsteen drown out worry about my father's health. By the time I've pulled into my driveway, I've convinced myself that Dad is being needlessly pessimistic about the likelihood he'll soon have another stroke. He's probably developed some mathematical model to predict his odds, but he leaves out a factor that can't be calculated: the love and support he gets from Natalie and me and the kids. That's got to improve his health.

I step into my house and embrace cheerful chaos for the next three hours—feeding the kids, playing with the kids, bathing the kids, and finally getting them settled into their beds. Sean doesn't arrive until the battle is almost over, so we postpone our dinner until after the twins are asleep.

"You worked late, but you seem more cheerful than yesterday," I observe as we feast on a meal of pasta washed down with cheap pinot grigio.

"We turned up security camera footage of Terry's fight. It shows the other guy pushing him first, so I'm hopeful the DA will realize he can't make an aggravated assault charge stick. We'll see." Sean twirls pasta around his fork. "But guess what? When I called my mom to tell her the news, she told me she knows Dermott O'Shea, our bow hunting victim."

"Really? How?"

"He was a member of her church. They were on some committee together." Sean takes a swig of wine. "You know how my mother is always trying to match up all the single people she knows. When she met a single man in his fifties, it was like finding a lump of gold in the street. Naturally, she pumped Dermott on his personal life. Turns out he used to be a priest."

"Did he leave the priesthood for a woman...or a man?" I ask.

"Neither. He told my mother he didn't feel he had a vocation, so he took a job with that charity. But he was still very devout. Went to mass every day. Mom was very impressed."

"So you think that's significant?"

Sean shrugs. "It gives me a new avenue to explore trying to learn more about who O'Shea was and who might have a beef with him. I've got someone else working on the archery angle—clubs, competitions, recent purchases of bows and arrows. Tomorrow, I'm going to the church to interview the priest and anyone else in the congregation who might've known O'Shea well."

"What about the blood on the arrow? Are the test results back?"

Sean studies me over the rim of his wine glass. "The blood on the arrow is O'Shea's. The arrow you found must've been the first one shot. It scraped his face. At first the pathologist doing the autopsy assumed he scraped his face on a branch as he fell. But the first arrow must've winged him before the second arrow took him down."

I pause with a forkful of salad suspended above my plate. "So if two arrows were fired at the poor man—"

"That means he was definitely murdered."

Chapter 24

For the third time since the Dupree sale, Ty is late to work. Today, he didn't even bother with vague excuses like "I have an appointment." He just texted, "in by 11." Donna's out running errands, so I'm all alone in the office.

It's not like we're swamped with work since we failed to land the last two jobs we bid on, but he was supposed to take the load of donations to Sister Alice in Newark today. If he doesn't leave until afternoon, he'll be stuck in rush hour traffic on the return trip.

I'm mildly annoyed, but I have more important things on my mind. Celeste Dupree continues to ignore my calls and emails. My father hasn't yet reported in on his exploration of Jeff's computer, and I know better than to nag him. I can't call or visit Katherine Dupree. I'm at a standstill in my quest to discover who bought the reliquary.

Unless...

I look longingly at the Google search bar on my computer. I can try to track down Matthew or Daphne Singleterry. Celeste said, "leave the Singleterrys to me," but then she took off for California. She's clearly dropped the ball, and I think I'm justified in trying to pick it up and run with it. Celeste might be justified in keeping me away from her mother, but she has no influence over what I do with Jeff's children.

A Google search of the two Singleterry siblings brings up nothing. It doesn't surprise me that they're not on social media as they both seem quite anti-social. I know Matthew rents a room in a house, so his address isn't popping up. But what about the video game world? Could I track him down through his participation in online gaming?

I could if I knew anything about it. I close my eyes to summon up all the young men I might know who play video games. Eventually, I come up with my neighbor's perennially under-employed son. He spends most of his days lounging in her basement rec room, so she's always offering him up to anyone who needs help with yardwork or household chores. Sure enough, I have his cell number in my contacts since he once shoveled snow for us. I text him with what

I need to know, offering him twenty bucks if he can come up with a contact for Matthew.

He responds with surprising speed. Apparently, Matthew Singleterry is fairly well known in the online gaming world. My neighbor offers to send Matthew a message through a game platform since he can't secure a phone number or email. I ask my neighbor to tell Matthew to get in touch with me and give him my number.

Within half an hour, my phone chirps with a text.

It's Matt. Do you have news on my money?

My money. Hmmm. What did Celeste tell him to expect? I type my reply.

I need to talk to you. Have you heard from Celeste recently?

Bitch keeps blowing me off. Where are you?

At my office. When are you free to come over?

I can leave right now. Give me the address.

Now that I've found Matthew, I suddenly have qualms about his eagerness to meet with me. Perhaps I should tell him to come later when Ty is here.

Whenever that might be.

No, I'm going to strike while I have the opportunity. I give him the office address and sit back to wait.

By ten, Matthew is at my door. When I let him in, I'm taken aback by what a wreck he is. Dressed in a thin hoody not warm enough for the crisp late October weather, Matthew sniffs through his red, drippy nose. A cloud of sour body odor clings to him as if he hasn't had a shower in days. He plops down in a chair before I invite him to sit. "Well? Have you gotten that auction place to give the reliquary back?"

Sliding into my swivel chair, I study Matthew from across the desk. "No-o-o. Did Celeste give you the impression that was possible?"

Matthew thumps his knee with his fist. "I told her that thing belongs to me and Daphy. You and Celeste and the old lady are all in this together. You stole my father's reliquary and then tried to buy us off with a paltry twenty grand. We want the reliquary back. We want to sell it ourselves."

Did Celeste even try to convince Matthew that we didn't rip him off? I start from scratch explaining Katherine's plan to give him and Daphne money and the role she asked me to play. "She told me she didn't want to insult you with a handout, but I think she also wanted to give you the money behind Celeste's back. She didn't want to argue with her daughter about it."

"That's bullshit!" Matthew shouts. "She's never given a rat's ass about us. She wanted to steal that reliquary."

I keep my voice calm and low. "Matthew—think it through. If Katherine had known it was in the cottage and wanted to steal it, she would've taken it out of your dad's house as soon as he died. She wouldn't have let it go into the estate sale."

Matthew draws down his brows. I can see he's having a hard time letting go of his grievance. He'd rather believe his own illogical narrative.

While he's mulling over my explanation, I start asking questions. "Did your father ever mention the reliquary to you?"

Matthew shakes his head. "My father never talked to us about all that medieval crap. He knew we weren't interested like the Duprees were. They were *intellectuals*, after all." Matthew juts out his jaw to deliver his scornful judgement. "Although sometimes he talked to Daphy about the herbal stuff—she's into those quack home remedies."

"Do you know how your dad got the reliquary?" I ask.

Matthew's eyes flare. "How could my father buy such a valuable thing when he never gave my mother one red cent for child support?"

"I've been wondering the same thing."

Jeff's son rubs his damp nose with the back of his hand. "He must've stolen it."

I'm shocked by how easily Matthew leaps to the conclusion that his father was a thief. "If he stole it, then you and Daphne really aren't the rightful heirs."

Matthew lurches forward in his chair. "Well, that guy who bought it for five bucks and resold it doesn't deserve it either!"

If Matthew can't have the money, he wants to make sure the buyer also doesn't get it. Spite is a small consolation prize. "I've discovered one person who knew your father had the reliquary—a Professor Healy from the College of Saint Joan. Do you know him?"

"Nah. My father didn't have friends other than the Duprees. If you want to call them friends." Matthew rises. "If you want to know about other professors he might have known, you should talk to my mother. She's a history professor, too."

Jeff's ex-wife—there's a good lead! I get the contact info from Matthew and send him off, irritable but somewhat mollified. Maybe he feels better about not getting the proceeds of the reliquary sale now that he suspects his father didn't honestly own the thing. He seems to want to uncover "the guy who bought it for five bucks." Interesting that he used the word "guy." Why would he assume it was a man? More women attend estate sales than men. Could Jeff have had a lady friend? Would Katherine have cared? Not that Jeff had much to offer a woman in the way of nice dates, but he wasn't bad looking, and older women always complain about slim pickins.

I think about Matthew for a while after he leaves. He's suspicious and paranoid and thinks the worst of everyone, especially the Duprees. Why does he hate them?

⸺⸺◈⸺⸺

TY ROLLS IN AT 12:30. Instead of the track suit and sneakers I'd expect him to be wearing to haul donations to Newark, he's dressed in black slacks and a pale blue button-down shirt.

I lift my eyebrows. "Did someone die?"

Ty throws back his shoulders. "A man can't come to work looking like a respectable adult?"

"Not when he's scheduled to haul dusty furniture to our favorite nun." I point to the pile awaiting him.

Ty knocks the heel of his hand against his forehead. "Shit. I forgot all about that."

"Ty, what's wrong?" I close out my spreadsheet and peer at him from across my desk. "You've seemed very distracted recently."

Ty's gaze slides away from mine. "I, uhm—"

"Tell me."

He runs his hand over his head. "I wasn't ready to talk about it yet. But I got a deal brewin'"

I tilt my head. "What kind of deal?"

"I wanna own my own business, Audge. You know I gotta side hustle with Carter pickin' up some extra cash by attending auctions of 21st century art for him. And I bought a painting and resold it for a nice profit a few months back."

"Fantastic! You never told us about it."

Ty waves away my compliment. "That kinda wheelin' and dealin' is too risky. I got lucky and made some cash. But I coulda lost just as easy. It's stressful, know what I'm sayin'? I want something steady, reliable."

"Uh-huh." I want to tell him that owning your own business is always stressful and never entirely reliable, but I don't want to rain on whatever news he's trying to share.

Ty paces across the office. "Anyway, the art deals have allowed me to build up some dollars in my account. And then—" He takes a deep breath. "The business opportunity I've been planning for kinda dropped into my lap."

Now he's got my attention. Ty has talked intermittently about owning a business someday, but it seemed more like a pipe dream than an event we both had to plan for. My throat feels dry. "What opportunity is that?"

"A self-storage business out near Dover. I've done a lot of research, and I know that's the kind of business I want to operate. Low overhead, minimal staffing. And Lord knows, there's a limitless number of customers who can't bear to toss out their junk." Ty grins and makes a raking motion. "Bring it to papa!"

Now Ty's bouncing with excitement, and I don't want to deflate his bubble. But I'm worried. Can he really afford to buy a business? Does he have the skills to run it successfully? No one is a harder worker than Ty, but he's only thirty.

Same age as I was when I started Another Man's Treasure.

"Well, this is certainly...exciting," I say. "Why did you keep the news on the downlow for so long?" Honestly, I'm a little miffed. Didn't he want my advice?

"I was gonna tell you soon." Ty has the grace to look sheepish. "I wasn't actively searching for a business to buy yet, but I went and visited this guy in Dover a few months ago as part of my market research. He started his storage business from scratch—it's not a franchise—and I wanted to learn how he did it. Then a few weeks ago he called and said he got some bad health news and wanted to sell and was I interested."

Hmmm. I hope this guy isn't unloading a turkey on a naïve young man.

"I know you probably think I jumped at the first opportunity, but I didn't," Ty says. "I got comparables on other businesses. I talked to Isabelle Trent about the value of the property, and I had Mr. Swenson review the contract before I signed anything. And I hired your tax accountant to audit the books."

"Wow! That's what I would've told you to do." So why not tell me about it instead of sneaking around behind my back? The question hangs unspoken between us.

Ty bites his bottom lip. "This is so hard, Audge," he says, his voice barely above a whisper. "You've taught me so much. I wouldn't be where I am today without you. But—" he gazes at the pile of donations awaiting his attention. "It's time, ya know? I gotta be my own man, gotta prove to myself that I got what it takes to succeed."

I feel light-headed. Ty is leaving? *Quitting*? "I didn't realize," I stammer. "I mean, I guess I knew somewhere in my head that you wouldn't work here forever, but I didn't think it would be—" My voice trails off.

So soon. Right now.

"I'm sorry," he whispers.

"No, don't be sorry. I'm proud of you," I say once I'm confident I can hold my voice steady. "When will you leave?"

"Not for a while, Audge. Don't worry." Ty squeezes my hand. "There's still a lotta stuff that has to happen with the bank and the lawyer and all the paperwork. I'll be here through the holidays. And Imma find you a great replacement and train him up right."

I offer him a shaky smile.

A replacement for Ty.

As if.

Chapter 25

One day after Matthew's visit, his mother has agreed to see me. She has reverted to her maiden name, Bernadette Clausen, and teaches history at Ramapo College, a half hour drive from Palmyrton. I find her in a small office crammed with books and papers on the third floor of a brick building in the center of campus. Her one window looks into the branches of a nearly bare tree where squirrels run up and down. She's somewhat squirrel-like herself, with fluffy grey-brown hair, plump cheeks, and a jumpy demeanor.

Bernadette clears a stack of blue essay books off a chair and invites me to sit. I already explained the purpose of my visit in a long introductory email, so I'm relieved when she starts talking without much prompting.

"I met Jeff when we were both associate professors of history at Rutgers. I admired the passion he brought to his subject—medieval religious history. He could talk about it for hours and he was quite fascinating...even entertaining."

She takes a deep breath, occupying her hands by clicking a ballpoint pen. "We started eating lunch together...then dinner. I was flattered by his attention. I've always struggled with my weight," she runs a hand along her hip and then up through her mop of frizzy curls, "and my hair. Jeff was so intellectual; it was like he didn't even notice my appearance."

She falls silent for so long, I feel the need to prompt her. "You got married, and..."

She jumps, surprised to find herself in the present day with me in her office. "Yes. It was rather impulsive on both our parts. We were both paying too much for apartments we hated. We realized we could buy a small house if we combined our resources, and being married made it easier to get a mortgage."

How romantic.

"Jeff insisted on a City Hall wedding. My mother was disappointed but relieved that I was finally getting married at thirty-eight. It wasn't until after our marriage that I understood the depth of Jeff's antipathy toward organized religion."

I tilt my head. "But he spent his days studying the lives of the saints."

Bernadette nods. "For Jeff, the Middle Ages was a period when people's faith was good and pure. Not like today."

"What changed his perspective?"

Bernadette leans back in her chair and gazes at the ceiling. "Something that happened long before we met, something he never told me about until there was a crisis in our marriage."

Again, she seems to have drifted off into the winds of time. "A crisis?" I nudge.

Bernadette clears her throat and begins speaking. "At first, we were happy in our marriage. We spent our time at home reading, researching, talking about history. Unlike me, Jeff really didn't like teaching. He had no patience for undergraduates with all their slacker ways and excuses for shoddy work. His true love was research. But associate professors are expected to carry a heavy teaching load. One semester, Jeff was assigned a graduate course. He was thrilled because the class was small and the students serious. One of his students was a young priest earning his PhD." Bernadette massages her temples. "Every day, Jeff came home and complained about him. Jeff ridiculed him in class, graded his work harshly, accused him of plagiarism, and ended up failing him. Naturally, the young priest complained. There was a huge uproar. Other professors reviewed the young man's work and found it excellent. Jeff was fired."

I lean forward, intrigued by this possible adversary. "What was the priest's name? Why did Jeff pick on him?"

Bernadette throws up her hands. "I can't recall his name. This happened over thirty years ago."

But I won't let it go. "Was his name Dermott O'Shea? Does that ring a bell?"

Bernadette scratches her head. "Dermott is an unusual name. I feel like I've heard it recently."

"He's the man who was shot in Hamilton Park by deer hunters," I explain. Of course, I leave out the part about it being murder. "He was a former priest."

Bernadette looks utterly baffled. "What could that possibly have to do with Jeff?"

What indeed? But it's clear Bernadette is not following my leaps in logic. "I'm sorry. You were telling me about Jeff's student who was a priest. Continue."

She leans across her desk and locks her gaze with mine. "I demanded to know why Jeff had singled out a priest. By this time, I was pregnant, and now my husband was unemployed. I wanted an explanation." Bernadette resumes clicking her pen. "At first, Jeff stonewalled me, but then Gaston Dupree convinced my husband to tell me everything."

"Jeff confided in Gaston?" Celeste had given me the impression that her father was too busy for his old friend.

"Not so much, later in life. But they went through a lot together as kids. Gaston and Jeff both attended a small Catholic high school for boys in Rhode Island. Jeff entered the monastery as an observer the day after graduation. He knew nothing of the world. He was an only child, raised by a devout widowed mother who was thrilled by his decision to become a monk. Jeff didn't want to be a parish priest. He envisioned living in a monastery and devoting himself to prayer, study, and service." Bernadette leans her forehead on her hands. "That's far from what he got."

She takes a deep breath and continues her story. "Before Jeff could move on to the next step in monastic life—becoming a postulant—he became aware of liaisons between some of the older postulants. He was so naive, he thought they just had special friendships. Then one night, he was sexually assaulted by a postulant. He escaped without being raped, but he immediately complained to the abbot." Bernadette pulls back her shoulders. "And do you know what that man did?"

"Hushed it up so there wouldn't be a scandal," I offer.

"Exactly. And Jeff was asked to leave the monastery. Told he didn't have a vocation."

Bernadette gazes down at her folded hands. She seems genuinely sad for her ex-husband, even after all these years.

"He had to return home in shame to his disappointed mother. Naturally, he couldn't tell her the truth—she wouldn't have believed monks could behave that way. His vision of monastic life was shattered. He became violently opposed to all organized religion. But he was still a man of faith and a scholar.

So he devoted himself to studying medieval religious history and earned his PhD."

"Did he admit he had an irrational reaction to the priest in his class?" I ask.

Bernadette offers a rueful smile. "Jeff was never very good at admitting he was wrong about anything. However, once I heard the whole story, I understood, I was sympathetic. But Jeff's getting fired and my giving birth to the twins sent our marriage into a spiral." Again, she gazes out the window as if she's gone back in time.

I give her some space for her thoughts, but my clock is ticking. "He had trouble finding a new teaching position?"

"Yes, but that was just part of the problem. You see, Jeff and I had agreed when we married not to have children. I thought I was infertile because of a medical treatment in my twenties, so I had accepted living life childfree, and I didn't see the need to use birth control. When I conceived, I was shocked but soon felt delighted. Jeff did not share my enthusiasm. He wanted me to terminate the pregnancy. I refused."

I keep my face impassive but inside I'm shuddering. Daphne and Matthew weren't exaggerating when they said their father didn't want them.

"My mother said he'd fall in love with our twins as soon as he saw them," Bernadette continues. "But that didn't happen. Everything about parenthood irritated Jeff—the crying, the mess, the constant neediness of babies." She gives a bitter laugh. "It's not like it was easy for me, either. I needed to keep working full time, and I got no help at home from my husband."

I can't imagine what our life would be like if Sean didn't enjoy being a father. "That would be a nightmare," I agree.

"All Jeff ever wanted to do was think, study, and pray. Our home life became the antithesis of his ideal existence because...well, because it was nothing like a cloistered monastery. So we divorced, and I had sole custody of our children."

Bernadette's lip trembles. "I tried my best, but both my children have problems. They were terribly damaged by their father's rejection."

I know a thing or two about rejecting fathers, but I've recovered from my own traumatic childhood. I'm curious why Daphne and Matthew struggle so much. "Did you ever tell them what happened to their father in the monastery?"

"Yes, I explained it to them when I felt they were old enough to understand. It didn't help. They feel their father chose his books and his research over them, just as the children of addicts feel their parents chose drugs over them."

"But they did visit him occasionally, as adults?"

"Mostly to try to guilt him into giving them money." Bernadette snorts and rolls her eyes. "He never paid me child support when they were little, and I knew it was pointless to hire a lawyer to garnish his wages. You can't get blood from a stone. But Matthew and Daphne never stopped trying to make him pay."

"People often equate money with love," I say.

"Jeff had neither love nor money to offer his kids. He was penniless—worked as an adjunct professor and wrote scholarly articles, neither of which pays a living wage. Jeff would've been living on the streets if Gaston Dupree hadn't rescued him and let him live in that cottage."

I suspect it was actually Katherine who rescued him. I wonder how Bernadette feels about her? "How well did you know Gaston and Katherine Dupree?"

"I met Gaston when Jeff and I were dating. I found him intimidating and imperious, but Jeff had no trouble standing up to him. They'd engage in long debates about arcane points in philosophy and theology. I didn't care to join in."

"You didn't socialize as two married couples?"

Bernadette utters a bitter bark of laughter. "The Duprees traveled in different circles. Even when he was in his thirties, Gaston was already quite successful as an architect. Before he built the house in Palmyrton, they lived in Manhattan. Threw stylish parties...ate at fancy restaurants. Not my scene."

I recall the stunning photo of Katherine as a young woman that I found while setting up her sale. I can't imagine that she and frumpy, awkward Bernadette would be fast friends. "But Jeff was friendly with Katherine as well as Gaston?" I enquire gently.

Bernadette's lips form a tight line before she speaks. "I imagine he must've been. Later...when we were divorced, and she was ill."

Hmmm. I hear a hint of jealousy there, even after all these years. Bernadette doesn't seem all that thrilled that the Duprees threw Jeff a lifeline.

Which brings me to the heart of why I'm here. He was particularly interested in the veneration of saints."

"Who are those scholars who also studied saints? Do you know their names?"

"No, of course not. That's not even close to my field."As I leave, one final question pops into my head, and I turn around to ask it. "Bernadette, do you know what order of priests ran the monastery that Jeff attended. Jesuit? Franciscan?"

She answers without hesitation. "Benedictine. The monastery belonged to the Order of St. Benedict."

Chapter 26

On my way home from my visit with Bernadette, my mind spins with theories.

Could Dermott O'Shea be the priest that Jeff treated unfairly in his classroom all those years ago? He's the right age to have been a grad student thirty years ago. Were they still adversaries, or had they become friends now that Dermott had also left the priesthood? But if he and Jeff had reconnected, why would Dermott be walking in the woods near Jeff's house after Jeff was already dead? Was it just a coincidence he was there on the day of the sale?

Next my mind turns to Jeff and how he acquired the reliquary. If Jeff had never traveled abroad, and never bought and sold artefacts, then there are only two ways he could have acquired the reliquary. One, if another scholar gave it to him. Or two, if as Matthew suspects, he stole it.

Given Jeff's prickly disposition, it seems unlikely that someone bestowed a valuable gift upon him. So could Jeff have stolen the reliquary from the monastery that expelled him? I picture Jeff as a religious young man suddenly stripped of his idealism by the sexual intrigue at the monastery and summarily dismissed. It makes sense that he might grab the reliquary on his way out the door.

But wouldn't the monks put two and two together if their reliquary disappeared at the same time Jeff was expelled? I ponder that issue while stuck at a traffic light. It may be they didn't immediately notice the thing was gone –after all, it's small and not that spectacular. Also, they'd have no way to accuse Jeff of the theft without getting into the reason he was expelled.

Now, over forty years later, the sale of the reliquary has been in the news, but possibly the story hasn't reached an order of Benedictine monks in Rhode Island.

Or maybe it has, and they're still unwilling to come forward and admit why it was stolen.

Or maybe no one there now remembers anymore.

All I have to do is find that monastery.

SEAN STAGGERS DOWNSTAIRS damp but happy after giving the kids their bath and reading *Madeline and the Gypsies* five times in a row. "I think Pepito is going to end up in juvie by the time he and Madeline are old enough to drive," he says, plopping down beside me on the couch.

"Don't be so pessimistic. He's just high-spirited."

"Humph. You women all go for the bad boys when you're young."

"And then we wise up." I kiss his cheek. "Except for poor Bernadette Clausen. She married monkish Jeff Singleterry when she was thirty-eight, and she still ended up dumped and alone with two kids." I fill Sean in on all I've learned today and show him the screen of my laptop. "Now I'm searching for Benedictine monasteries in Rhode Island. Seems like there's only one."

Sean looks at the image of Saint Benedict on the homepage of the Monastery of Saint Giles. "Good ole Saint Benedict. They tried to poison him when he wanted to reform the bad behavior of the monks in the monastery he led. He defeated the poisoners twice. Then everyone considered him a miracle-worker."

I twist to face my husband. "How in the world do you know that?"

"I dunno. Musta been beat into my head by Sister Mary Immaculata in fourth grade, along with all kinds of other useless information I've retained from my parochial school years."

"Poison." I turn the concept over in my mind. "You know, everyone speculated Jeff died from taking too much of one of his herbal remedies. But what if he were intentionally poisoned?"

"Au-dreee." Sean's eyes will get stuck in his forehead if he rolls them any harder. "Why would anyone want to poison a poor old history professor?"

"For the same reason they tried to off St. Benedict—maybe Jeff knew about someone's bad behavior and wanted to shine a light on it."

Sean frowns. "A minute ago, you were accusing Jeff of having stolen the reliquary. Now you think he's some kind of holy avenger."

"Yeah, but he stole the reliquary for a reason. The monastery where he was studying was corrupt. Jeff reported the sex abuse to the abbot and got expelled for his efforts. Maybe he wanted to get St. Benedict's remains to a more holy place." I take a deep breath and hit my husband with the other part of my theory. "What if the young priest that Jeff mistreated in his class was Dermott O'Shea? What if Jeff and Dermott had reconnected? Doesn't it seem weird that two men who'd each aspired to a religious life and failed, died within a few hundred yards of each other?"

Sean shakes his whole body like a Labrador retriever emerging from a lake. "Jeff's death was accidental."

"Was it?" I grab my husband's hands. "Seriously, Sean—why did they do an autopsy on Jeff Singleterry? Was there a suspicion of foul play?"

"Not necessarily," Sean props his feet up on the coffee table. "There's a lot of gray area when an autopsy is ordered. Obviously, there's an autopsy if there's any suspicion that the death wasn't from natural causes. So if a 95 year old person with multiple health problems dies in bed, there's no autopsy. But if a young, healthy person dies in bed, there would almost always be an autopsy. They'd suspect drugs, so that would be crime-related."

"What about a generally healthy older person?"

Sean shrugs. "Probably not. That's the gray area when it's up to the investigating officer." Sean leans against the kitchen counter. "Say for instance a 60-year-old Muslim man dies suddenly. The family is heartbroken. In the Muslim faith, you're supposed to bury the body within three days, so the family doesn't want an autopsy. In that situation, we'd most likely let it go."

"But the family might've killed him," I protest.

Sean laughs. "Highly unlikely unless there's other evidence. And autopsies are expensive, so you don't order them up for everyone."

"So back to my original question. Why did they do an autopsy on a poor 72-year-old man who died in his bed with nothing suspicious going on? Wouldn't that normally be one that the police pass on?"

Sean lifts one eyebrow. "Yeah...probably." Then he snaps his fingers. "There's always an autopsy if you're going to be an organ donor. Maybe that's why they did it."

I smile sweetly at my husband. "Would they have saved tissues from the autopsy? Is it too late now to test for exactly what compound killed Jeff?"

"I don't know what they save," Sean grouses. "But I do know they can't run a limitless number of tests. The pathologist has to have some idea of what to look for in order to confirm or deny it's there. A standard tox screen is for common drugs that people OD on. They're not going to look for every funky herb under the sun that might cause kidney damage."

"What if an estate sale organizer happened to take pictures of the herb bottles she found in the victim's kitchen? What if the stalks of the herbs the victim grew were still out in his garden? Then could they check?"

Sean laughs. "Maybe. But it would take months for the results to come back because it's not a top priority. And a cop would have to order the tests. And it would be charged against his budget. So it's not going to be me."

I sigh and chew on my cuticles.

"Why do you care so much?" Sean asks.

"What if we could prove Jeff Singleterry was murdered? Wouldn't the police be able to get a court order for Christie's to release the name of the seller?"

"Whoa, Audrey! That's a tall order!"

"All I asked you is a hypothetical question. Would the police be able to get Christie's to talk if it's part of a murder investigation?"

"Sure, but—"

I turn out the kitchen light and head for our bedroom. "The first step is to find out why they did the autopsy and what the findings were. Then all I have to do is prove Jeff's kidney failure was no accident."

"Good luck with that."

———◉———

THE NEXT MORNING, I'M working from home. After I get the twins fed and dressed and settled with their toys, I call the Monastery of Saint Giles in Rhode Island. Eventually I'm connected with a Brother Raphael, a delightfully chatty fellow who doesn't have a suspicious bone in his body. It's as if he's spent his entire life just waiting for my call.

We quickly establish that Jefferson Singleterry was never a postulant there. Before I can swallow my disappointment at another dead end, Brother Raphael offers new information. "Perhaps the man you're looking for studied at the Monastery of Saint Regis. It was a smaller Benedictine Community that merged with ours after a fire in the seventies."

"A fire! What happened?" Surely Jeff didn't torch the place on his way out?

"Careless carpenters repairing the roof of the chapel. A discarded cigarette butt ignited some sawdust after the men went home for the day. By the time the fire was discovered that evening, it had consumed the entire interior of the chapel and started to spread to the living quarters. Luckily, no one was hurt, but the building was a total loss, so the remaining postulants and brothers came and joined our community."

"And the records of who had studied there in the past?"

"All went up in flames, I'm afraid."

"Are any other of the original brothers from Saint Regis still living in your community?" I ask.

"Only Brother Linus. He's 101, God bless him. Sadly, he suffers from dementia."

I know this is a total longshot, but there's no harm in asking. "Did Brother Linus ever mention a reliquary that belonged to the Monastery of Saint Regis?"

"The reliquary! Now how in the world do you know about that?" Before I can form a response, Brother Raphael plows forward with his own story. He seems like a person who so rarely gets an opportunity to talk that he's eager to use every possible moment. "It was the abbey's most precious treasure because it contained a fragment of the bone of St. Benedict himself. It was rescued from a small church under bombardment in Italy during World War II. A returning soldier brought it to Rhode Island and presented it to the monastery. Tragically, it was lost in the fire. Brother Linus still talks about it—his mind lives far in the past."

The reliquary sold at Jeff's estate sale is the same one Brother Raphael and the other members of his community believe was lost in the fire. It has to be! But there's no way to prove it. The only person alive who saw the reliquary years ago has dementia now. I resolve not to stir anything up with the brothers until I have time to think through my next steps.

"Thank you so much for talking to me, Brother Raphael. This has been so interesting. I've gotta run—my kids are calling for me!"

I hang up and look at Thea and Aiden playing happily on the rug. I'm going to burn for lying to a monk!

Chapter 27

Later in the afternoon, my father shows up at my house. I'm surprised to see him since he no longer drives and takes Ubers whenever he's not with Natalie. "Sorry to pop in on such short notice." Dad adjusts the straps of a worn backpack on his shoulders. "I was on my way home from my acupuncture appointment, and I thought I'd stop by to tell you what I've discovered on Jeff Singleterry's computer."

I kiss his cheek as I usher him into the house. "I hope you can stay for a while. The kids just went down for their nap."

"That's fine. It will give us some time to talk without distraction. I'll stay until they wake up." He sits down and opens the backpack, removing a file folder filled with typed notes. Dad clears his throat and begins as if he were back on campus, delivering a lecture to his mathematics grad students.

"I noted two themes in Jefferson Singleterry's academic articles. One concerned the treatment of various painful intestinal ailments that medieval persons attributed to divine retribution for sins, but which were actually caused by consuming contaminated or spoiled grains." My father glances up from his notes. "I found it fascinating that some of the herbal remedies actually did work although not for the reasons the healers believed. Anyway, Singleterry wrote frequently on the use of wormwood. Taken in high doses, it can be toxic, so I suspect these medieval healers killed more of their patients than they saved, but luckily for them, there were no ambulance chasing lawyers in the twelfth century."

Dad flips one page of notes over and moves on to another. "Next, I noted the theme of holy relics, such as those contained in reliquaries, as a form of veneration for a saint." Dad glances up over his glasses. "Singleterry made a strong point that veneration is not the same as worship, which is reserved for God. However, the relic of a saint could be venerated, which is an expression of love for the saint stemming from admiration of his or her life and work. And this veneration could sometimes lead to miraculous healing. Or so the faithful believe."

Dad offers no commentary on how outlandish he, a man of science, finds this, but the expression on his face speaks volumes. I hesitate to admit to him that I think it's fascinating, but I share what I've learned from Brother Raphael.

"Good work, Dad. Since I last talked to you, I've learned more about the reliquary. I'm pretty sure it contained a relic of Saint Benedict, who was known for two things. First, he was a reformer who established rules of good order for monasteries. And when some monks wanted to get rid of him by poisoning him, he escaped their efforts twice by working miracles."

Dad arches his eyebrows. "He was simply smart enough not to eat anything they offered him."

I smile at my father's relentless logic. "Probably. But what you've discovered in Jeff's articles explains his passion for the reliquary. He would naturally admire Saint Benedict for being a reformer of monastic life. And maybe since Jeff worked with herbs, he thought proximity to the holy relic would protect him from poisoning."

"Which it clearly didn't since he you say he accidentally poisoned himself," Dad says, pushing the folder of notes across the table for me to keep.

Or was poisoned by someone else. But I'm not going to get into that with my father. It's bad enough Sean thinks I'm stretching probability; I don't need my father's disapproval as well.

He straightens his back and folds his hands. "I also found something else that may be of interest to you, Audrey. One of Jefferson Singleterry's academic articles had a co-author."

"That's not unusual, is it?" Some of my father's own articles had several collaborators.

"Papers in the sciences and mathematics often have long lists of collaborators. It's not as common in the humanities, but not unheard of. However, this article was the only one of Singleterry's that had a co-author," my father explains. "The title is, 'The Role of Reliquaries in Atonement for Sin.' The co-author is a Professor Jeremiah Healy, of the College of St. Joan right here in New Jersey. The article was written three years ago, and Singleterry and Healy discuss in great detail a reliquary said to have contained remains of Saint Benedict. That's your reliquary, correct?"

My heart quickens with excitement. "Yes. I've spoken to Healy. He gave me the impression that the reliquary wasn't that significant and didn't interest him as much as it did Jeff. Now you're saying Healy actually collaborated with Jeff in writing about the reliquary. Why would he mislead me?"

Dad gives my question serious thought. "Perhaps he wanted to divert your attention. He must have assumed that you'd never notice an article in an obscure historical journal. But I would say this lie calls into question the veracity of everything else he told you."

"Right. Including his insistence that he'd never been to Palmyrton and was tutoring the day of the estate sale." Professor Jeremiah Healy will soon be coming under my close scrutiny.

"Has this been helpful?" my father asks.

"You're a genius, Dad! But we've always known that."

Chapter 28

Dad is still at our house playing with the kids when Sean arrives home. Overwhelmed by a bounty of attention, Thea toddles to her father while Aiden elects to stick with Gampa. I allow ten minutes for joyful greetings before launching into the primary reason for my father's visit. "Dad found out that Jeremiah Healy collaborated with Jeff in writing about the reliquary. He's clearly seen it. He lied to me."

Sean chuckles. "Welcome to my world. Perps lie all the time."

I jump on his terminology. "So you agree that Healy is a perp? You think he bought the reliquary?"

Sean laughs, but I'm not sure if he's laughing at me or Thea, who is hanging off his arm like Spanish moss on a live oak. "Okay, I know buying the reliquary doesn't make Healy guilty of a crime, but there's more. Today I talked to the Monastery of Saint Giles in Rhode Island. Jeff was never a postulant there, but he might have studied at a smaller Benedictine Monastery that burned down. And that monastery had a reliquary, which everyone believed was destroyed in the fire."

Now I have my husband's attention. "What's that word you used? Post..."

"Postulant. It's the second level of becoming a monk," I explain.

Sean moves Thea to the floor and leans closer to me. "Yeah, that's what I found out today when I took my mother to church and met all the people there who knew Dermott O'Shea. Turns out, we didn't have our facts exactly straight. Dermott was never a priest. He was a whattayacallit—postulant—at a Benedictine Abbey, but he left before he became a monk. Decided he didn't have a calling."

"Whoa! I didn't ask Brother Raphael if Dermott had studied at Saint Giles. He couldn't have been at the smaller monastery because he's twenty years younger than Jeff, so it would have been burnt down by the time he entered monastic life."

My father listens to this exchange while helping Aiden fit shapes into his sorter box. "You still have no evidence that the two men had reconnected," Dad reminds me.

"Nothing solid," Sean agrees. "But all the parishioners I talked to today agreed that Dermott seemed excited or restless in the last few weeks of his life. The old biddies attributed it to romance, but I suspect it might have something to do with discovering the reliquary."

"You didn't find any letters or diaries at Dermott's house to give you a clue what he was up to?"

Sean ruffles my hair. "Only mystery authors find clues in diaries. I've never known a cop to find a diary."

"Maybe we're trying too hard to find a significant connection," Dad offers. "The two men could have run into each other at the Palmyrton ShopRite."

Sean frowns. He doesn't like coincidences. But Dad has given me an idea. "We know that Jeff lived in Palmyrton because the Duprees offered him a place to stay. What brought Dermott to Palmyrton? You said he had no family here. He worked for a small, local charity—not the kind of position a man would move for."

Sean runs his hands through his short, sandy hair. "And he ended up dying in a park no one had ever known him to visit before." He crinkles his nose and scoops up Aiden. "Something around here stinks, and it's not just this investigation."

Dad insists on taking an Uber home so Sean and I can focus on feeding the kids and putting them to bed. While we work on that, we keep talking.

"I think you should talk to Katherine Dupree tomorrow now that we're pretty certain there's a connection between the reliquary and Dermott's murder. Celeste has kept her walled off at Shadow Glen, but your badge ought to get you in."

"Thank you, Audrey. I'm so grateful to have a supervisor here at home to take over when Chief Gaskill is not available."

I nudge him with my hip. "Sorry. I didn't mean to be bossy. It's just that our two mysteries are converging."

Sean places his hands on my shoulders. "They are. Which means that you should devote yourself to running more estate sales and let me handle the investigating."

"Well, better get a move on it. Because until I can show the world I didn't screw up in selling that reliquary, new estate sale customers are going to be hard to find."

Chapter 29

The next morning, Ty enters the office right on time.

"I'm so glad you're here. I want to see if you recognize this man." As I call up the College of St. Joan website to find Prof. Healy's photo, I fill in Ty on what I've learned. "Healy told me he'd never seen Jeff's reliquary, never been to Palmyrton, but the academic article makes it clear that he had examined the piece. I foolishly believed him because he seemed so dismissive of Jeff Singleterry." I pound my computer keys. "And if he lied about never seeing the reliquary, then he could've lied about not coming to the estate sale. He said he was tutoring that day, but we can corroborate that if you can ID him."

I click on tabs for "faculty" and "Art History," and a photo for Healy pops up. He's surprisingly youthful—a guy in his thirties with a full head of hair and a broad smile. Funny, he sounded older on the phone. Ty squints at the photo. "Doesn't look familiar."

Donna comes to look over our shoulders. "His bio says he joined the faculty in 1998. That could be a really old photo." She sniffs. "Their website isn't very sophisticated. They probably rarely update it."

"Good point," I agree.

"I'll google him," Donna offers. "Hmm. Here he is on Facebook, but he uses a picture of his dog as a profile pic. Aha—it says he graduated high school in 1986, so he's in his fifties, not thirties like the picture on the college website."

"Where can we find a current picture to show Ty?" It's frustrating to be so close.

"He also pops up on RateMyProfessor.com." Ty points at the computer screen. "That's the site you go to see if your professor is a psycho before you sign up for his course," Ty explains. "Sometimes it's BS—kids just raggin' 'cause they got a bad grade. But if a lotta people say the same thing, then I'd pay attention."

Ty, Donna, and I gather around the computer as Donna zooms in on the profile photo—a fiftyish man with large, horn-rimmed glasses and a close-cropped salt and pepper beard.

Ty tilts his head one way and the other. Damn! He's not recognizing the guy.

Then Ty lays a finger across Healy's glasses, and a slow grin spreads across his face. "Oh, yeah! At the sale he wasn't wearing glasses and he had one of those goofy bucket hats pulled down low. And his beard was solid black."

"He could have darkened it with temporary dye," Donna says.

"But that's him. He bought the reliquary, the garden tool, and the mug." Ty shuts his eyes, "I can picture him coming up to the table and just kinda sliding the stuff over to me. He didn't say a word."

Relief washes through me. Finally, we're getting somewhere!

"Let's read his profile on Rate My Professor," Ty says. "He's got a 2.5 average rating out of five. That's not too good."

We scroll through the reviews.

"Has a mean sense of humor. Makes fun of students."

"Very condescending."

"Acts sneaky. Tries to trip you up when you answer a question."

"Cancels class on short notice."

"Knows a lot about art. Interesting."

"Liar! Said he went to Harvard but he didn't."

"Sounds like his students agree with my perception of him," I say. "But even if he knew Jeff had the reliquary, how did he know about the estate sale that day?"

Donna opens another window of her computer. "He's obviously into art. Maybe he's on our customer mailing list. We've got over 7,000 names." We watch as she types Jeremiah Healy's name into our mailing list database.

Ping! jhealy@stjoancollege.edu

Ty pounds the desk. "Man, we invited the fox right into our henhouse!"

"We couldn't have known," Donna answers. "The email announcing the sale talks about all the fabulous stuff in the Dupree house. There's just one little sentence at the end that mentions the contents of the caretaker's cottage are also included in the sale."

"Ugh! I added that," I moan. "I thought it would help us get the smaller house cleared. But if Healy had collaborated with Jeff on that article and had seen the reliquary, then he would have known that the caretaker's cottage on the Dupree property was where his friend lived."

"He took a gamble that the reliquary might be in the sale," Ty says. "Came out here real casual-like and hit the jackpot!"

Chapter 30

"Call Carter Lemoine," I command Ty.

Carter is our closest contact at Christies even though he had nothing to do with the reliquary auction. But since he and Ty often work together on 21st Century African American art, Carter immediately accepts Ty's call. Ty puts the art expert on speaker phone after explaining that we think we know who bought and resold the reliquary.

Carter chuckles. "Sounds like you've done some excellent detective work, but I'm afraid you can't call Christie's with your guess and expect us to confirm or deny it. We respect an auctioner's right to privacy."

I recall Celeste's theory that we could pressure the buyer by proving he knew what he was buying. But that was when I thought I needed to claw back the money for Matthew and Daphne. Now that I'm quite certain Jeff stole the reliquary, all that matters is redeeming the reputation of Another Man's Treasure.

"Yes, but what if we can prove the reliquary was stolen and should never have been in the estate sale in the first place," I insist.

Carter makes a tsk-tsk sound. "That's a more serious matter. Naturally, Christie's wants no part in auctioning stolen goods. But the parties from whom the piece was stolen would have to make that claim and show proof of ownership. Not the estate sale organizer who accidentally sold it."

"Damn," Ty says after we've hung up. "That old monastery went up in smoke. Who could you find to make the claim that it belonged to them?"

"No one." I sit in silence for a while.

"What are you thinking?" Donna asks suspiciously.

"When you really consider it, the Monastery of Saint Regis didn't own the reliquary any more rightfully than Jeff Singleterry did. It was brought to them by a soldier who supposedly rescued it from a bombed church in Italy. It technically belongs to that church, which may not even exist anymore."

"And who knows how they got it," Donna adds.

"Exactly," Ty agrees. "That little box has been kickin' around from place to place for seven hundred years. We're just one stop on its long journey."

Ty's words strike a chord in me. I rise and pace the office. "Isn't that a great story? Remember, getting the reliquary back isn't our goal. And helping the Singleterry siblings no longer matters—they don't have the right to inherit a stolen artefact. Our goal is to redeem the reputation of Another Man's Treasure." I wag my finger at my staff. "We can do that ourselves by telling the complete story of the reliquary and how it came to be in the shabby cottage of a poor, discredited academic."

Donna bites her lower lip. "You mean, like, write a press release about it, or do a blog post and share it on our socials?"

"Yeah." I sit back down at my desk and pull my laptop toward me. "I'll work on a first draft and you two can help me jazz it up."

Donna trades a look with Ty. "Uh, Audrey—I don't think the story will get much attention if it comes from us. We're just an obscure estate sale company in New Jersey."

Ty nods. "Yeah, the story of the sale went viral because Christie's promoted the rags to riches angle, and it got picked up by the network news." He rubs his fingers together. "Money always makes headlines."

I slump in my desk chair. "You think it's hopeless? No one will listen?"

"The story truly is fascinating," Donna admits. "We just need to package it better. Get someone with more clout to tell it."

Ty pulls out his phone. "Carter's got connections at the *New York Times*."

And that's how I come to turn over all my notes to a reporter on the art beat, just in time for the holidays.

I've done all I can do. I'm letting Sean handle his job investigating Dermott O'Shea's murder. I'm letting the *Times* reporter tell my part of the reliquary story. And I'm devoting myself to planning Thanksgiving because this year it's our turn to host the entire Coughlin clan.

Chapter 31

Two weeks later, I survey the wreckage of my home on Thanksgiving evening.

Recently occupied by thirty-two feasting Coughlins plus Dad and Natalie, the first floor of our house now looks like the aftermath of a battle between the Visigoths and the Huns. The skeletons of two turkeys, one roasted, one deep-fried, sit on the kitchen table. A blodge of cranberry sauce forms a bloody pool on the tablecloth. China plates, our own plus those borrowed from my mother-in-law, are stacked waiting to be processed through the dishwasher like corpses of the battle dead.

"Tell me again why we can't use paper plates for holiday meals?" I ask my sister-in-law, Deirdre, who has graciously stayed behind to help us clean.

She wrinkles her nose. "Gravy soaks through paper." Deirdre passes through the dining room and living room with a plastic wash basin, collecting forks, knives, and spoons. "I'll take all the silverware home, wash it in my dishwasher, sort it, and return yours to you tomorrow morning. Here's four spoons for your breakfast."

"How have you survived doing this every year for fifty years, Deirdre?" I wipe the bottom of my bedroom slipper after dragging it through a sticky wad of pecan pie that hit the floor beside the kids' table.

"I don't think of it as *survival,* Audrey. Family holidays are fun."

"Even the part where Terry drank four beers in half an hour and threw a punch at Brendan, forgetting that Brendan is the brother footing the bill for the attorney defending him on robbery charges?" Sean asks his sister as he tosses out the remains of the green bean casserole.

Dierdre sniffs. "Terry is not himself these days."

"Not himself" is the euphemism all Coughlins use to excuse bad behavior, big and small. Uncle Pat was also not himself when he accused me of being a liberal hellbent on destroying America, nor was Cousin Timmy himself when he yanked a toy truck from Aiden's ten-years-younger hands, setting off a cataclysmic tantrum.

"Should I save these sweet potatoes," Sean asks me as he continues to scrub his way through the kitchen as if his life depended on eradicating baked-on grease.

"Only if they don't have marshmallows." I pass him on my way to haul yet another garbage bag to the can in the garage. In addition to holiday stress, Sean is under a lot of pressure at work because there still has been no break in the Dermott O'Shea murder case.

Deirdre slams shut the twenty folding chairs that she'll be taking back to her house. "She seems awfully tense," I whisper to Sean as I head back out to the dining room to help her.

"She's still upset that I haven't done more to get Terry out of his jam."

I don't reply. We've already talked the Terry situation to death. Sean's brother will either take a plea or stand trial. Either way, he'll have a felony conviction, which will make it even harder for him to get and hold a job. All the Coughlins are distraught, and somehow they blame Sean for being the arresting officer rather than blame Terry for committing the crime.

Out in the dining room, Deirdre continues to fold and stack. "It was nice to see your Dad today, Audrey." She pauses momentarily. "Is he feeling okay? He kinda zoned out when I was talking to him."

I turn away from her shrewd nurse's eyes. "He gets a little overwhelmed by all the Coughlin noise. He's a bit hard of hearing, you know."

She nods and lets my explanation pass. I feel a stab of fear because I also noticed my father's blank stare just as dessert was being served. But, I reassure myself, he was perfectly fine before and after.

The three of us load the chairs into Deirdre's SUV. "Thanks for everything, Sean and Audrey. We'll all be back in three weeks for the twins' birthday!"

As I watch my sister-in-law's taillights disappear into the night, I turn to face my husband. "There's no freakin' way we are having all thirty-two of them over here on Christmas Eve for the twins' birthday."

"We did it last year," Sean says.

"That was their first birthday. We simply can't do it every year for the next eighteen years. I'll lose my mind."

"Yeah, me too. But how can we deprive them of a party?"

"The kids? Their birthday is Christmas Eve—they'll be over the top with excitement for that. I think we should start celebrating their half-birthday in

June with a party outside. Then we can keep Christmas Eve nice and cozy with just us and my parents and your parents."

Sean nods. "Okay. But you tell them."

Chapter 32

"Sushi!" Ty calls as he sails through the office door with a white shopping bag at lunchtime on the Monday after Thanksgiving.

He sets it on Donna's desk and starts unpacking. "Spicy tuna roll, California roll, monster roll."

The right side of Donna's top lip curls up and she averts her head. "No thanks. I'll stick with the turkey sandwich I brought from home."

Ty's hand freezes over the carry-out bag. "Whattaya mean, you're eatin' turkey? You never turn down sushi."

This is a strange development. I study Donna's face, which looks torn between desire and mild revulsion. I remember a time two years ago when I felt the same way about tacos. A lightbulb goes off. "Donna, are you pregnant?"

Donna's eyes open wide. "How did you know?" She rests her hand on her tummy. "I'm starting to show already, aren't I?"

In fact, I had noticed that Donna had gained a few pounds, but I wrote it off as newlywed bliss. "Pregnant women aren't allowed to eat raw fish. I knew you'd never turn it down for any other reason." I jump out of my chair and head toward Donna as Ty stands with his mouth hanging open.

"I just found out," she says. "I don't want to tell everyone so soon."

I hug her. "Congratulations! I'm sorry I guessed. I'll keep your secret."

"Imma be an uncle again!" Ty beams.

"We thought it would take a while, given my age." Now that the cat is out of the bag, Donna seems eager to talk. "So we threw away my birth control pills in Greece. But wham—I think it happened as soon as we got back."

I stroke her hands. "That's fantastic. You'll be the best mother in the world."

"When's the baby due?" Ty asks.

"July 15." Donna grins. "I've already started cleaning in preparation."

My genuine happiness for Donna hits a speedbump. Ty leaving in January...Donna on maternity leave in July. And what if she doesn't want to return to work? How will I manage?

Then again, maybe I'll have nothing to manage. The dearth of business caused by the reliquary debacle has now segued into the usual holiday lull in estate sales. What if business doesn't pick up after New Year's? The *New York Times* article about the reliquary still hasn't appeared. Clearly annoyed by my repeated inquiries, the reporter told me with considerable frost this week that she'd notify me as soon as her editor scheduled the feature.

Okay, I get it—the life and times of a medieval reliquary will certainly be reserved for a slow news day. But I'm so eager to read her interpretation of the story. I know she's interviewed Celeste and Matthew and Daphne. They aren't aware that I'm the one who proposed the idea for the story; Celeste simply asked me if the reporter had talked to me, and Matthew and Daphne seemed to relish the attention. Of course, the reporter must've talked to Professor Healy as well, but I haven't heard from him. I'm dying to know how he reacted to being exposed as the buyer.

I snap back to reality when I hear Donna telling Ty that she'll find out the baby's sex at her next doctor's appointment. "Then I can start painting the nursery," she adds.

"If it's a girl, don't go overboard with the pink," Ty advises. "You don't want her to grow up to be a princess."

"Speaking of princesses, Thea had a meltdown this morning when Aiden pulled the ear off her bunny." I hold up the severed appendage. "Could you perform surgery, Donna? You're so much better than I am with a needle and thread."

Ty shoots me a look. "Better? You know you'd just staple that ear back on if we left it to you."

"I admit I failed Home Ec." I keep talking as Donna sews. "Here's another Bad Mommy moment—Thea and Aiden aren't having a big birthday party this year. I can't endure another Coughlin family blow-out, so I'm keeping the party to grandparents only."

"Makes sense," Ty says.

"But I have to break the news to my mother-in-law."

"Eeeew," the two of them chorus.

"Let me know if you want to role-play," Donna adds. "I've got plenty of experience with hysterical mothers."

She puts the final stitch into Bunny's ear and lays him on my desk. "Good as new."

Chapter 33

Deciding I'll bite the bullet and stop by my in-laws' house today, I leave the office early. On the way there, I pass Whole Foods and pull in to shop for Aiden's favorite organic cereal. It seems I've become the kind of mother who makes special trips to procure obscure food products for her picky eater. As I walk down the cereal aisle, my eyes riveted to the shelves in the quest for Multigrain Spoonfuls, I crash my cart into another shopper's cart.

"Oh, I'm so sorry!"

The man startles, but instead of being annoyed, his face breaks into a grin. "Oh, wow—fancy meeting you here! I was just thinking of you yesterday."

It's Bob Geary, the hiker who was an early bird at the Singleterry sale, still wearing his trusty backpack.

"Remember me?" he asks cheerfully as he blocks my cart with his own.

"Of course, you were at the Singleterry sale. Bob, right?" I finally spy the blue box of cereal I'm seeking and reach for it over Bob's head. "Why were you thinking of me?"

I'm not sure I want to know, but I'm positive he's going to tell me.

"As you can imagine, the hiking community is in quite a twist over the shooting in Hamilton Park. We're astonished that the police still haven't arrested anyone, so my friend and I were doing a little armchair crime-solving recently." He draws an imaginary Venn diagram in the air. "There's quite a cross-over between true crime enthusiasts and hikers."

Good lord, this man can talk! "Is that so?" I spy some jam we like on the other side of the aisle and toss it in my cart just to remind him I'm here to shop, not jawbone with him.

"Yes, indeed. My friend and I were speculating on why that poor man, Dermott O'Shea, was in the woods that day. And I told my friend, 'I know he was going to the estate sale.'"

I interrupt Bob. "Actually, he wasn't. None of us saw him there. He didn't buy anything."

Bob nods in agreement. "That's because he was killed before he got there."

I can't help but chuckle at his confidence. "And how can you possibly know that?"

"Because—" he shrugs off his backpack and pulls out an old book, "I found this in the book I bought at the sale." He flips the book open to a place he's marked with a sticky note and hands it to me.

Now he has my full attention. I take the book from him and read Jeff's tiny, precise writing in the margin. *Only D. can help me return the relic.*

My gaze travels to the paragraph in the book beside which Jeff wrote his note:

Although many holy relics are the prized possessions of individuals, their miraculous power is magnified when they reside in a place of worship where they can be freely visited and venerated by pilgrims seeking aid.

I close the book to see the title: *Holy Relics and the Miracles they Wrought.*

I peer at Bob Geary there in the breakfast aisle of Whole Foods. "You think Jeff intended to give the reliquary to Dermott O'Shea so he could return it to a monastery?"

"See—I knew you'd catch on!" Bob is delighted by my conclusion. "D is obviously Dermott, and Dermott was an ex-monk. But Jeff died before he could hand it over. So Dermott came to get it at the estate sale, but sadly, he never made it there."

I feel my jaw hanging down. Goofy Bob Geary has come up with a plausible theory for Dermott O'Shea's murder. Of course, he doesn't know what I know about who actually bought the reliquary. Could Jeremiah Healy have killed Dermott to prevent him from getting to the reliquary first?

"But why shoot him with a bow and arrow?" I'm thinking aloud, not challenging Bob's theory. "Archery is a rather specialized skill."

Bob takes the book back from me and flips it open to another page. This one contains a reproduction of a medieval drawing showing a man standing rather nonchalantly with his body pierced by scores of arrows. "That's Saint Sebastian. Looks like a pin cushion, right? He was the patron saint of archers and athletes and those who desire a saintly death." Bob arches his eyebrows in case I miss the significance. "He was shot by arrows for converting people to Christianity and left for dead. A widow found him and nursed him back to health." Bob shakes his head. "Too bad poor Dermott didn't have one of those."

A shiver passes through me. Katherine is a widow who likes to nurse strays.

The caption under the illustration tells me that St. Sebastian was a popular subject of Renaissance artists. His relics are in a Basilica on the Appian Way in Italy and were visited frequently by pilgrims in the Middle Ages and continue to be visited today.

Who else would know this stuff except Professor Jeremiah Healy?

"I showed this book to the police, and they were totally uninterested," Bob complains.

"What cop did you tell?"

"Just the fellow sitting at the front desk of the Palmyrton police station. He wouldn't send me up to talk to the detectives."

I take the book from Bob. "Don't worry. I'll see this gets into the right hands."

Chapter 34

Sean shows considerably more interest in the book than did the desk sergeant downstairs who sent Bob away. My husband immediately sends someone to bring in Jeremiah Healy for questioning. And he himself plans to return to Shadow Glen to talk to Katherine Dupree.

Again.

"Thanks for bringing this in. I'll call you when I know something." He brushes his lips across the top of my forehead. "Go on home and take it easy."

Right.

The discovery of the book has pushed all thoughts of a conversation with Sean's mother out of my mind. I leave Sean's office and drive home lost in thought.

The first time Sean talked to Katherine, right before Thanksgiving, he got in to see her with no problem, but she told him nothing. Although she admitted she knew the reason why Jeff had left the monastery as a young man, she insisted that he'd never mentioned taking the reliquary. She steadfastly maintained that she didn't know he had it, didn't know Dermott O'Shea was the student who'd ended Jeff's teaching career, and didn't know Jeremiah Healy. Sean had been certain Katherine was unnerved by his questions, but she couldn't be shaken from her story.

Sean came home defeated by an elderly aristocrat in a wheelchair.

This time, I know he's determined to find out who would know about all these subtle allusions to the lives of the saints. Whoever killed Dermott, and possibly Jeff as well, was sending a message.

Was Katherine the intended recipient?

After leaving yet another voicemail for the *Times* reporter, this time telling her big news is about to break, I pace restlessly around the house waiting to hear from my husband, while Roseline tends to the twins.

I notice Thea tugging her ear. I hope she's not getting an ear infection, but she doesn't feel feverish.

"Here's your mail." Roseline places a pile of junk mail and bills in front of me. "Looks like you got your first Christmas card of the season."

Sure enough, there's a square greeting card envelope addressed in beautiful script mixed into the junk. Gosh, I hate people who get their cards out before December 1!

The card has no return address, but that flawless handwriting tugs a memory somewhere deep in my brain.

I open the envelope. Instead of Santa or snowmen, the card has a lovely reproduction of a dreamy watercolor—blues and greens and purples with a slash of red and gold. Flipping it over, I see the title of the artwork. "Sunset in the Mountains, Watercolor, Katherine Dupree, 1972, Hartford Museum."

Huh. Katherine was a painter. I didn't know that. I open the card, which is filled from edge to edge with tiny, precise handwriting. Not a Christmas card after all.

Dear Audrey,

I am sending you this letter in a feeble attempt to make things right between us. All my life, I have impulsively followed my heart, leaving a trail of destruction in my wake. In my clumsy efforts to set some matters straight, I've inadvertently created more chaos for you and for my children.

What an odd opening. What is Katherine leading up to? I read on.

In order for you to understand why I was trying to give money to Jeff's children, you must understand my relationship to Jeff. We were once more than friends. I will not attempt to justify my infidelity other than to say that Jeff needed me in a way that Gaston never did. Gaston never suspected a thing. He considered Jeff so insignificant that he couldn't imagine a woman choosing Jeff over him. Unfortunately, it was Todd who discovered us together. He was so young, he didn't even understand what he was seeing. So he told his sister.

She understood all too well. And told her father. Poor Todd always regretted that because he liked Jeff.

In the midst of all this drama, I received my diagnosis. And from that moment on, my future was determined. I couldn't leave Gaston. He'd never let me take the children, and I had no way to support them or myself. No way to get the medical care I needed. And Jeff certainly couldn't support us all. Indeed, he didn't want that responsibility. He never wanted children.

My disease was my punishment.

I set the letter down again. Man, this is heavy stuff! Imagine believing you got a crippling disease as retribution for infidelity! If that happened to everyone who cheated, half the population would be in wheelchairs! Indeed, Gaston himself deserved a disease.

When Katherine wrote this, she was unaware that Todd had told me about Gaston's infidelities. Katherine and Gaston married in a romantic whirlwind, and once the passion died down with the arrival of kids, Gaston must've kept up the high-flying lifestyle on his own while Katherine, home alone, turned to their old friend Jeff for comfort. What a mess! But why does Katherine feel I need to know all this? I resume reading.

So we were separated for many long years. Years in which Jeff married, had children, lost his job, and divorced. And then fate brought us back together again. I was at the Metropolitan Museum of Art with a friend and encountered Jeff there. He began visiting me at home. This time, I didn't hide it from Gaston. I presented Jeff as a solution to the problem of finding reliable caregivers for me. You see, Gaston enjoyed his public role as the noble, loyal spouse of a cripple, and Jeff allowed him to keep playing it with very little effort.

We enjoyed a few years of true happiness. Or, I should clarify—I was happy. Jeff continued to carry a burden on his soul. He said there was an evil he needed to correct before he died. He wouldn't tell me more than that.

Hmmm. Was it atoning for his treatment of Dermott O'Shea? Or perhaps his failure to find the reliquary a suitable holy home.

Then Jeff died, just as suddenly and unexpectedly as Gaston.

I knew that he'd died without correcting the evil because he was still talking about it a few days before he passed. I assumed—wrongly, as usual—that he wanted to achieve some reconciliation with his children. I never knew anything about the reliquary, and I have no idea of how Jeff obtained it, but I suspect now that he must have stolen it.

I knew Daphne and Matthew felt abandoned by their father, wounded that he'd never supported them. I knew Jeff had a hard time connecting with them because they didn't share his passions. So I thought I'd give them the money and say it was his last wish that they have it. I needed you and your business to help me achieve that goal, and I dragged you into the scheme without your full understanding.

I thought my action would bring everyone peace.

Instead, it has sown more heartache and strife.

Please use this letter as proof that you are blameless in what happened. I will not be available to testify on your behalf.

Please forgive me,

Katherine Dupree

What does she mean by, "I will not be able to testify?" Immediately, I call Sean to give him a heads-up, but he doesn't answer. He's probably already at Shadow Glen.

I call Katherine's cell phone and listen while it rings endlessly and finally rolls over to voicemail. Rather than leave a message, I call Shadow Glen where I know residents have landlines in their rooms that connect through a central switchboard.

My request to be connected to Katherine Dupree's room is met with a long silence. "Who's calling?" the woman on the other end finally asks.

"Audrey Nealon. I just received a card from her, and I wanted to check to see if she's all right."

Another silence. "Please hold."

Anxiety eats away at my gut the longer I wait on hold. Why can't they simply connect me? Finally, the line clicks and an authoritative voice speaks. "I'm so sorry to inform you that Mrs. Dupree passed away two days ago. I understand from the family that the services will be private."

"But wait...what happened?"

"I suggest you contact her daughter Celeste with any questions." Click.

Does Sean know Katherine is dead? Surely, he must if he was just at Shadow Glen. But what does this mean? Did Sean's last interview with her upset her so much that she.... No, maybe she just passed away from natural causes.

My heart hammers. I really need to know. I can't believe Sean didn't call me on his way back to the station. If that's where he is.

I call his work landline and some other cop picks up. "He's interviewing a suspect. Can't be disturbed."

He must be grilling Healy.

Okay, fine. I guess I have to sit here and wait for news.

Thea comes over and leans her head against my knee. "Mama, bunny."

Roseline performs a pantomime behind Thea's back. "Did you bring Bunny home?" she mouths.

My stomach drops. Oh, crap! I left Bunny at the office after Donna fixed him.

"Mama, bunny," Thea repeats with more urgency, tugging her ear.

"Sweetheart, Bunny is resting after Aunt Donna fixed his ear," I offer, knowing this will never fly.

"BUNNEEEE! BUNNEEE!" Thea's shrieks pierce the air.

Chapter 35

I struggle to fit my key in the lock of the office door while juggling my tote bag and fumbling with the flashlight on my phone. Roseline offered to stay a little late with the twins while I make a mad dash to the office to retrieve Bunny.

The days grow shorter every November, yet every year we act like we've never experienced the phenomena before. "I can't believe how dark it is at five o'clock," we all murmur in shock.

But it's true. Last month at this time, I could see the keyhole in my door clearly. Today, it's shrouded in darkness.

Finally, after much blind scratching, I feel the key slide into the lock.

Get in, grab bunny, get out.

I feel a presence emerge from the shadows behind me. "Who—"

An arrow splits the wood of the door frame to my right. A hand covers my mouth before I can scream. The person pushes open the door and we both stumble through.

I'm too startled to be afraid.

That is, until I see the tall man dressed in black with a ski mask over his face and a hunter's crossbow over his shoulder.

He slams the office door shut and flips the deadbolt.

My racing heart sends blood pounding through my ears. This can't be happening. Was this guy watching the office, waiting for an opportunity to break in?

"What do you want?" I ask. "There's not much here but go ahead and take it. Just don't hurt me."

My kids need me. They can't lose me at age two.

The man starts talking, low and fast. I can't understand his words. In fact, he doesn't seem to be addressing me. Behind the mask, his eyes dart back and forth.

I wait while he paces and mutters. Bunny reproaches me from the desk. Why did I forget him?

But I'm not good at waiting. Never have been. I need to know what's happening here.

I raise my voice, trying to sound confident not bossy. "What do you need from me? I just came here to pick something up. My family knows where I am, and they'll come looking for me soon."

"Shut up!" the man screams. Then he goes back to muttering.

How long will it take before Roseline starts to worry? How long will she worry before she takes action? Who will she call? Sean can't be reached. He's with Healy.

Or is he? Is this Healy? I've never met the man, only seen his headshot. I have no idea how tall he is.

I need to keep this guy calm. Whoever he is, he took two arrows to kill Dermott O'Shea out in the woods, but he'll only need one for me in the narrow confines of this office.

He paces frantically; I squeeze myself into a corner to stay out of his way. More time passes with no change, and once again, I can't help myself. "Would you like a soda," I offer inanely. "There are some cans in the fridge."

"I don't drink soda! It's not healthy!"

Who's concerned with health? Bob Geary or one of his true crime fanatic /hiking buddies? Maybe I underestimated him and let him set me up.

I'm afraid to say anything about Jeff, or the reliquary, or the Duprees for fear I'll provoke him. But I want to hear him speak again. I sense I've heard that voice before.

"I have two kids," I say. "Twins—Thea and Aiden."

"Twins. Jeff has twins." He keeps pacing. "They're stupid. Jeff doesn't like them. He likes me. He talks to me. I'm like Saint Sebastian. The archer. I've always been the archer."

And then I know. I think about the sports trophies Donna threw away at the Dupree sale. She said the Dupree kids must've gotten them at camp. Archery is something kids do at summer camp.

This is Todd Dupree. Ty said he talked to himself when he came to Jeff's cottage. Celeste implied her brother was a little unstable.

A lot unstable, as it turns out.

I need to keep him talking. His eyes seem less frantic while he's taking coherently. Keep him talking until help arrives, as it surely will.

Eventually.

"Did Jeff teach you all about the saints?" I ask.

"Yes. All the saints. Especially Benedict. He was the most important one. He made the rules. I like rules. But Jeff broke the rules. That's why he couldn't keep Saint Benedict. I said he should give him to me. But Jeff said no."

Todd breathes heavily. That speech wore him out.

I think of my precious Thea, wailing at home. Collapsing from exhaustion as she waits for her bunny. I'm coming, darling. Please believe me.

"What did Jeff want to do with the reliquary?" I ask.

"Give it to Dermott to take to the monastery. That way all the monks would pray for Jeff. He needed prayers. He broke a commandment."

That would be the one about not coveting your neighbor's wife, I presume. "But you didn't want him to have the prayers?" I ask.

"No! And I stopped Dermott from getting Saint Benedict. Dermott used to be Jeff's enemy but then he became his friend. That didn't make sense to me. So I stopped him from taking the reliquary. But by the time I went back for Benedict, he was gone."

Healy bought the reliquary while Todd was stalking Dermott in the woods. What timing!

"Benedict didn't protect Jeff from the poison," Todd adds. "So maybe he doesn't work miracles anymore."

"Maybe not," I agree. "Maybe the reliquary is just a regular box now."

Todd tilts his head. "Is Saint Benedict here?"

"No. I never had him. But feel free to look around."

Luckily, Donna has the office totally free of clutter. Todd quickly satisfies himself that the reliquary isn't here. "Okay. Well, I'm going home now." He heads for the door as if he's just one of my regular customers.

"Back to Boston?" I ask.

"Boston? No, I live in a big house with lots of windows in Palmyrton. I live with my Mom and Dad. Good-bye."

Chapter 36

One week after Christmas and one month after the police arrest Todd Dupree for the murders of Jefferson Singleterry and Dermott O'Shea, the call comes.

I answer just as Roseline arrives to take care of the children.

"Audrey, I'm at the hospital with your father. He's had another stroke. You need to come right away." Natalie hangs up.

I don't recall the drive to the hospital. All I know is that I'm standing next to the man who was once Roger Nealon—brilliant, logical, fiercely loyal, deeply loving Roger Nealon.

Now, an IV runs into his pale arm and a small hose attempts to offer up oxygen to his shallow breaths. His eyes are closed, his mouth slack.

"They want to put him on a feeding tube, Audrey," Natalie says as she clutches my hand. "But I refused to permit it. Your father wouldn't want that."

"But, but—maybe he'll wake up. The feeding tube will give him a chance to regain his strength," I plead.

Natalie shakes her head. "I'm sorry, darling. He won't get better. The stroke cut off oxygen to his brain for nearly five minutes. We have to say our good-byes. Take some time alone."

I hold my father's fragile hand in mine and whisper all the things I've told him many times. I love you. I appreciate you. You're the best dad and best grandfather.

I'm sorry for the years we lost.

I'm so grateful for the years we regained.

I forgive you.

Thank you for forgiving me.

I'll miss you.

Then I cry for what will never be. He will never teach Aiden and Thea to play chess, never help them with their homework, never offer them advice when their parents are driving them crazy.

At least he got to celebrate their second birthday.

As my tears fall unabated onto his hand, I feel the fingers tighten and release.

I jump up and look at his face. "Dad? Dad! Can you hear me?"

Natalie enters the room and approaches the bed. She lays a practiced hand on Dad's cheek. "He's gone, Audrey."

We fall into each other's arms and weep.

———◈———

THERE IS NO QUESTION of a church funeral. Instead, two weeks after my father passes, we hold a Celebration of Life ceremony at the Rosa Parks Community Center where he volunteered, teaching the kids chess and helping them with their homework. So many people from every walk of Dad's life turn up, the custodian scrambles to find more chairs. Fellow professors, students, chess buddies, classmates from Tai Chi, neighbors, and everyone from the Parks Center—all have come to pay their respects. Sean's family turns out in full force, as do Donna, Ty, and Ty's grandma Betty.

Grandma Betty is accompanied by a statuesque Black woman whom I've never met before—I wouldn't forget that monumental bosom. "Audrey, baby, this is my friend Gloria. She's the alto soloist from the Baptist church choir, and she's going to sing for us today."

I'm touched but horrified—Dad would not want hymns at his service. But how can I decline without hurting this woman whom I love?

Betty sees the confusion on my face. "Now, don't you worry, girl. I know your father wasn't one for church. Gloria's going to sing the first two verses of "Amazing Grace". Ain't no mention of God or Jesus or nuthin' like that in there. It's all about grace, and forgiveness, and being lost and then finding yourself again. I know Roger believed in that."

Gloria takes a seat and waits patiently as person after person rises to pay tribute to my father. They talk about his brilliant mind, and they talk about his big heart. They pay tribute to his logic, and they recall pithy one-liners that made them laugh. They explain how Roger challenged them and how he encouraged them.

I'm so overcome by emotion that I can only stammer out a few words of gratitude and praise for my own father before Sean leads me away from the podium.

Then Gloria takes the stage. Nodding to the pianist, who sounds just the opening note, she takes a breath and begins to sing in a thrilling, rich contralto, every note vibrating with emotion.

Amazing grace! how sweet the sound,

That saved a wretch like me!

I once was lost, but now am found,

Was blind, but now I see.

'Twas grace that taught my heart to fear,

And grace my fears relieved;

How precious did that grace appear

The hour I first believed!

When she finishes, nobody makes a sound.

And then beside me, Aiden pipes up. "Like that song. Sing again."

Chapter 37

The weeks after my father's death pass in a blur. I do my everyday mother and business owner tasks. But in the middle of paying quarterly taxes or slicing grapes in half, I'm felled by a grief so profound that I can't even summon up tears to cry.

My father, the person who loved me best in the world, is no longer walking this earth.

Sometimes I still reach for the phone to ask him a question. Or I buy Brazil nuts, which I despise, because I know he likes them.

And then I remember.

He's gone.

To make matters worse, Natalie also is leaving, moving to Boston to be closer to her son.

At work, I worry when the phone rings and worry when it doesn't. The *Times* article was finally published once the reporter made sense of the final chapter—Todd's arrest and the reliquary's new resting place in a Benedictine Abbey in Italy. The collector who bought it at the Christie's auction decided to donate it to a monastery that regularly received pilgrims.

So Jeff got his wish after all, although no mention was made about the Italian monks praying for him ceaselessly. The article brought plenty of publicity for Another Man's Treasure, but I've had to turn away some of the work.

I haven't recovered my usual energy and enthusiasm, and we still haven't found a replacement for Ty. With herculean effort, Donna and I managed a medium-sized sale in February with the help of Lamar and Ty's sister Charmaine. But Donna is getting bigger by the day, and she can't spend long hours on her feet.

Today, I get another request for an estimate on a sale. But when I arrive at the woman's house, a solid center hall colonial with a well-equipped kitchen and a big, detached garage full of tools and yard care appliances, she begins back-pedaling.

"I'm not sure I want to do an estate sale," Barbara Lansdown says after listening to my pitch.

I brace myself, waiting for her to bring up the reliquary incident. Instead, she says, "Maybe I'll just give all this away before I move to Florida."

"Why would you want to give it away?" I ask. "I can easily get you eight to ten thousand dollars for everything you have here."

She glances out her front window where a pack of neighborhood ladies dressed in colorful track suits strides along. One of them points to Barbara's house with its prominent For Sale sign, and they all respond with great animation.

"I don't want those old bats coming through my house and pawing through my things," Barbara says. "Can't you find another way to sell it without opening up the whole house for a sale?"

This is a new request. "Well, I could sell all the big items on Facebook Marketplace and Craigslist, I suppose. But I can't make individual listings for all the small items. That would be too time-consuming."

Barbara's face lights up. "Okay—so sell the big stuff and give away the small stuff. Will you handle that for me?"

I ponder for a moment but can't think of a reason to decline. So I agree and return to the office to draw up a modified contract. Later that evening, as I tell Sean about it, I think of another advantage. "This sale for Barbara Lansdown will be a cinch for Donna. She can monitor all the listings from her sofa."

Sean gives me a distracted smile of agreement. Once again, the new police chief has scheduled Sean to patrol downtown Palmyrton after the bars let out on Friday night, and he's not happy about it. He bangs around the kitchen fixing us an early dinner before he has to leave for his shift. The twins have already eaten and we're letting them watch a video so we can have a little couple time.

"How long is this new patrol policy going to last?" I toss some cucumbers into the salad bowl, trying to stay out of the way of his chopping knife.

"Who knows?" Sean decapitates a stalk of broccoli with one blow. "Palmyrton's always going to have bars, and bars always produce drunks on the weekends. Nothing has changed since he instituted these patrols except that we managed to arrest the son of a city council member for public urination, and the chairman of the library board for singing "O Danny Boy" so loud he provoked a fight with a homeowner."

And of course, Sean arrested his own brother. But I don't mention that.

I foresee an endless string of ruined weekends—Sean exhausted from working nights, me exhausted from running sales, our relatives exhausted from filling in with childcare. "What are we going to do?"

Sean's mouth is set in a hard line. He doesn't say anything for a long time, but I can tell that something is in his brain, waiting to spring forth. I lay my hand on his arm. "Tell me."

He drops his chopping knife and faces me across the kitchen island. "Audrey, I've been offered a new job."

My eyes light up. "As a detective? What police department?"

"Not as a detective. As the head of security for a big corporation. Regular hours, no weekends or holidays. I can even work from home occasionally. And the pay—" He leans across the island and whispers an obscene number in my ear.

"Wow! But would you be happy with that kind of work?"

"I think it would be challenging. It's focused on preventing theft, keeping the facilities secure, providing protection when there are high-level meetings between the executives and investors." He scrapes a pile of onions into a sizzling skillet. "No more chasing low-lifes."

I'm trying to process all this information. "Wait—you've already gone on an interview?"

"Two," he admits. "The first one was Zoom."

"Why didn't you tell me?" Suspicion creeps into my voice. This is too good to be true. There's got to be a snare somewhere.

"You've had so much on your mind. I didn't want to upset you."

"Why would I be upset by good news?"

Sean flips vegetables in the pan with intense concentration. "The job's in Delaware."

"Delaware?" I'm so stunned, he might as well have said Bhutan. "We'd have to *move*? Leave Palmyrton?"

"It'll be good to put a little distance between us and my family, even though it's only two hours away." Sean avoids my gaze. "And with your dad passed and Natalie moving, well—"

I poke his massive bicep with my puny index finger. "Are you forgetting something, Sean? What about my career, my business, that I built for fifteen years right here in our hometown!" I slam the salad bowl onto the table.

"Audrey, we have to think about what's best for our family. We can't both keep working crazy hours and unpredictable schedules. You've been so stressed and overworked with Ty and Donna both leaving. I've been a cop for twenty years. I can retire with a pension, and then earn the security director salary on top of that." He takes my hands in his. "You wouldn't even need to make money."

"I don't want to be a housewife!" I jerk my hands away from his and stalk across the kitchen. "I worked hard to build Another Man's Treasure, and you want me to walk away like it's nothing."

"No, I didn't mean you should totally give up your career." Sean follows me, repentant. "I just meant, you could start over in Delaware, and you wouldn't need to bring in a lot of money right off the bat. My salary could keep us fine until you get a new business started."

"But I'll be just as busy and distracted with a new estate sale business as I am with Another Man's Treasure. In fact, it'll be worse because I'll have no referral network for clients and no—" I bury my head in my hands. I know I'm not *old* old, but I feel too old to start over.

"What if you started a different kind of business?" Sean suggests. "More like what that woman Barbara asked you to do today. Consult with people. Tell them honestly what they have that's worth selling and help them sell it online or through your contacts. Find a charity that does pick-ups to take the useful items, and subcontract with a junk hauler to get rid of the rest. A virtual estate sale, an estate sale without all the work of an actual sale. Just think—no weekends consumed by sales."

He makes it sound so easy. I toss my head. "Just because Barbara asked for that service doesn't mean there's an actual market for it."

"Create a market." Sean serves the chicken-vegetable stir-fry onto our plates. "Get ahead of the curve. If anyone can do it, you can."

"Thanks for your confidence, but you don't know what you're talking about." I yank my chair away from the table and flop into my seat.

But Sean won't let the idea go. "You've lost jobs in the past when the homeowners decided they didn't want neighbors and strangers trooping through their house and picking through their stuff at an estate sale." He leans back in his chair and points his fork at me. "You'd be offering clients a way to privately sell items with significant value and give away the rest. Best of all, you'd have a business with no overhead. No staff to pay, no office to rent, no van, no insurance." He folds his hands across his chest and grins. "Just you and your computer and your phone."

Sean's phone starts to ring. "They need me at the station." He shovels three more bites of dinner into his mouth. "Think about it."

━━━◉━━━

I THINK ABOUT IT WHILE I give the twins their bath. I sink ships and make the shark swim and I know I can never make a virtual estate sale service work. Too many variables...too little profit. How dare my husband act so blasé about how easy it would be for me to start from scratch?

I think about it while we're snuggled in bed reading books. As I recite the misadventures of Curious George for the third time, I see a possibility in selling larger items through Facebook Marketplace and popular collectibles via eBay. But what about—

"Mama, turna page!" Thea demands, and I realize I've left George stuck in the jungle. I return to reading, but different business scenarios keep popping into my head.

I think about it when I'm downstairs alone with a glass of wine. I start Googling. I make a list of people to call. I set up a spreadsheet.

Sean finds me asleep on the sofa with a calculator in my hand when he returns at three in the morning. "Running some numbers?" he asks with one sandy eyebrow cocked.

Dragging myself upright, I mutter, "Yeah. It might work. Possibly. Maybe."

Sean grins. I can see he thinks he's won the battle.

Chapter 38

I'm running an estate sale at my own house.

Not really—it's just a really big garage sale to get rid of all Aiden and Thea's outgrown baby paraphernalia, the lumpy bed in our guest bedroom, the hideous chair from Sean's bachelor apartment, and all the ugly and useless gifts anyone has ever given us in our lives.

Gone.

No regrets. No guilt.

Isabelle Trent comes to the sale. She cheerfully got us top dollar for our house, but she grows weepy when she sees Thea's pink bassinet carried off by a pregnant woman.

"Isabelle! It's not like you to be so sentimental," I tease.

She dabs at the corner of her eye, careful not to smudge her mascara. "I know, but I'm really going to miss you, Audrey. You always make me laugh."

I loop my arm around her shoulders. "You're just worried that no one here in Palmyrton will be able to help you declutter a house in order to sell it."

She squeezes me tight. "You can do it long-distance with your new business idea. Best of luck, darling!"

Other friends and neighbors stop by throughout the sale, so it devolves into a drunken cocktail giveaway party as we unload the last items on unsuspecting passersby. The sun sets and we come inside to order pizza. Gradually, Lydia and Roz and Madalyn drift off. Sean's work buddies tip up their beer bottles and head home. Soon it's just Donna, Ty, Sean, and I trading stories about epic estate sales of the past.

"Remember the time you got locked in the secret room?" I ask Ty.

"How about the time they were ready to start knockin' down the house with you still in it?" he shoots back.

Sean points to Donna who has dozed off still holding her can of seltzer. "I'll drive her home," he offers.

I wake up Donna to kiss her good-bye. "Call me as soon as the baby is born. I'll drive back up to visit."

Now Ty and I are alone. We look at each other and glance away, suddenly as shy as teenagers at the homecoming dance.

Ty lets his long hands drop between his knees. "Audge, what can I say? You saved my life, man. You honestly saved my life."

"You saved your own life. I just cheered you on."

He looks up. "You believed in me when no one else did. Even Grams had her doubts."

I take his hand. "I believe in you still. You're the most fearless man I know. You've given me courage when I needed it most."

Ty pulls me into his embrace. "Tell me we'll always be friends."

"Always."

———●———

THE NEXT DAY, WE LOAD the kids into the car after watching the moving van pull away with all our worldly possessions. Thea howled when she saw the movers carry her bed away, but we convinced her the separation was only temporary.

"We're going on a great adventure, just like Madeline and Pepito."

"Venture?" Thea asks.

"Venture!" Aiden shouts.

We strap them into their car seats as they pound the windows and kick their feet shouting, "Venture, venture, venture!"

Sean puts the car in gear, and I lay my hand over his. "We're going on an adventure," I whisper.

"Life has always been an adventure with you, Audrey. That's why I married you."

———●———

Other Books by S.W. Hubbard

Would you like to be notified when my next novel is released? Please join my mailing list by visiting my website: https://swhubbard.net

Thank you for following all of Audrey's adventures in the Palmyrton Estate Sale Mystery Series. If you enjoyed these books, I hope you'll try all my other series.

Hurt People, a family saga thriller

Life in Palmyrton Women's Friendship Fiction Series

Life, Part 2

Life, Upended

Life, at Last

Life, Revealed

FRANK BENNETT ADIRONDACK Mountain Mystery Series:

The Lure

Blood Knot

Dead Drift

False Cast

Tailspinner

Ice Jig

Jumping Rise

About the Author

S.W. Hubbard writes the kinds of books she loves to read: twisty, believable, full of complex characters, and highlighted with sly humor. She is the author of the Palmyrton Estate Sale Mystery Series, the Life in Palmyrton Women's Friendship Fiction series, the Frank Bennett Adirondack Mountain Mystery Series, and the new thriller, *Hurt People*. Her short stories have also appeared in *Alfred Hitchcock's Mystery Magazine* and the anthologies *Crimes by Moonlight, Adirondack Mysteries*, and *The Mystery Box*. She lives in Morristown, NJ, when she's not traveling and hiking with her husband and her rescue dog. Visit her at http://www.swhubbard.net.

Printed by Amazon Italia Logistica S.r.l.
Torrazza Piemonte (TO), Italy

56105902R00087